SHADOWS
FROM THE
BASEMENT

Jay Bower

SHADOW FOREST

PUBLISHING

Cover art by Matt Seff Barnes

Editing by Heather Ann Larson

For all the Cellar Dwellers.
Without you, the Basement is no fun.

Contents

Evisceration Liberation

Sweet, sensuous, seductive, sinful. Most days, I wavered between these powerful emotions. When my efforts were delayed, I grew anxious. The shakes kicked in. I envied meth addicts coming down from their high.

But I wasn't a monster. I was just a man.

My last kill lingered on the tip of my tongue, though it had been two weeks. Like a vapor dancing coyly with my desires, it teased incessantly, taunting me to find another. If I ignored my passion much longer, I would get sloppy with the next one. Losing focus meant possibly losing my prey. I was the master of the impulses throttling my brain. They were my slaves.

My prey that night was a colleague named Dr. Jewel Carrington. She mentioned something about going out that night, and I finally figured out where she was going.

Charcoal-colored clouds covered the sky, blotting out the full moon. A crisp breeze crossed the parking lot, bringing with it the musical thump from inside the bar. Someone had a hard on for the '90s, and I wasn't mad about it.

I glanced across the parking lot toward the dimly lit sign—The

Copper Kettle—a stupid name, but the college students loved the place. Its name came from a giant copper kettle used to brew beer; it sat behind a wall of glass inside the bar. They worshipped it like it was a prized cow or the golden calf. It was neither. I wasn't even sure it was functional. It had never been in use since I lived there.

A short line of students waited to get inside. I joined them and kept to myself, not engaging in conversation if I could help it. None of them knew how many I killed before. A perk to teaching at a large university was students dropped out all the time and no one knew why, nor did they notice.

The girl in front of me turned back and smiled. Bouncing blonde curls accented her smooth pixie face. Large blue eyes and… oh god, those lips, red and plump, they called to me. Something stirred within me. Was she the one and not Jewel? Once the feeling settled in my gut, there was only one release.

"Hi!" she said.

I offered a cordial greeting, already breaking my desire to keep to myself. Professors and students were discouraged from engaging in social behavior outside of a class setting, but I was willing to toss those suggestions aside. If indeed she was my prey, it wasn't like she would ever see the halls of the university again.

We chatted for a minute or two. Her name was Amber, an undecided freshman from nearby Brownsville. I noticed a cross gleaming around her neck like a talisman and noted as such. She smiled and turned back around, obviously bored with my repartee.

Rose-scented perfume swirled around me, the first indication my impulses were compromised. Amber waited for the bouncer to check her ID before entering. Staring down at her phone, she flipped through images of people's meals and an endless stream of funny cats. It was always damn cats. When they created the internet, I wonder if they ever imagined its primary function would be for porn and cats?

"The line's moving," I said in a gentle yet stern voice. I developed it over the years while teaching American History at Southern Illinois University. It often worked, gaining the attention of my students with little effort.

She looked up from her phone. "Cool, thanks." Her voice—had I been able to savor the sweet pitch of her voice much longer, no amount of restraint would have held me back. She stirred feelings within that I normally kept in check.

The line moved faster once a group of frat boys wearing matching light-blue pocket t-shirts made it past the bouncer after far too much giggling. I shook my head. I never liked their kind, no matter how well they did in class. Something about frat-boy juvenile behavior irked me, but they weren't my concern unless they got in the way.

I intended on finding Dr. Carrington. She taught medieval history, something I could do without, but I knew she would be vulnerable after her daughter recently ran away. What better time to strike?

I entered The Copper Kettle and took a seat against the far wall, under a buzzing Bud Light sign. The location offered a prime viewing position for the rest of the bar.

The waitress with blue eye shadow and too-tight leather pants took my order.

"Blue Moon on tap," I said, then waited for my prey.

Amber sauntered across the bar and slid onto a barstool. She wore a low-cut, tight red sweater, with a pair of black leggings. My wife tried something like them once, but her body wasn't built for it.

My eyes were glued to the gorgeous co-ed. I instantly inhaled a scent of rose, though if it was from her or from my memory, I didn't know.

A male student stumbled to my table, barely able to stand. "Dr...Dr. Huffman? Dude, nice to see you, bro!"

I squinted, trying to remember his name. Zack? Jack? Dustan? Did it really matter?

"Yes?" I replied.

"Dude, it is you. Bro, can I... I buy–" He nearly fell over but clutched the worn chair and saved himself. "A beer?" he finished.

"No, thank you. Why don't you get home? I do hope you're not driving."

Zack or Dustan, whatever the hell his name was, smiled. "Nah man, got a ride. Gonna be safe and shit."

Good. I worried about his shit. I was glad to know it was safe.

"Take care, then. Enjoy the rest of your night."

He gave me a goofy thumbs up and stumbled toward his friends two tables over. They scolded him for acting foolish, but they did use his name, Bryan.

I should've known; it was the same as mine. I remembered him then, a baseball player that tried to get me to change a grade last year because his eligibility hung in the balance. I refused. Yet here he was, ready to buy me a beer. Maybe I should've reconsidered his grade when I had a chance.

Bryan eventually puked all over his friends, though I was surprised it didn't happen sooner.

I scanned the bar for the lovely rose-scented girl, expecting to notice her bright-red sweater in the sea of black and gray. It took me a few moments, but I spotted her next to a tall table on my left. She giggled and batted her eyes. So luminous. So alluring.

Dr. Carrington crossed in front of her, and my heart raced. Both of them? Could I dare attempt two in one night? The challenge piqued my interest, and I sipped casually on my beer.

Dr. Carrington—Jewel—took a seat at a table against the far wall opposite me. One of the frat boys in the light-blue shirts approached her, and my dreams of two women in one night faded fast. They talked for several minutes while she drank a glass of red wine. When she was done, she left with the boy, his eyes wide and a cheshire grin across his face.

Sipping my beer, I let go of the lurid dream. Jewel would be another day. With the boy in tow, it was too risky. She would taste what I had to offer soon enough.

But the rose-scented girl, she remained in the bar, and my eyes remained on her. My luck hadn't fully run out.

Dark electronic music blasted over the bar's speakers, taking over from the '90s rock jams I had been enjoying earlier. The new music was a perfect soundtrack to my sinister intentions. I smiled, sipped my beer, and plotted.

The girl shifted on her feet, her gentle curves swaying to the beat. I imagined her arms draped around me, their warmth comforting and delightful.

The music suddenly changed, an old Halloween song playing loudly. With the holiday only days away, it made sense. I didn't celebrate the day. With its evil connotations and dark spiritual energy, it wasn't conducive to my beliefs. I was a principled man when it came to a higher power.

Downing the last of my beer, I stood to leave at just the moment the girl tottered toward the door. Could I really have been this lucky?

I followed her closely, holding the door open like the gentleman my mother raised me to be.

"Thanks," she said in her soft voice. "Oh hey, you're the guy from earlier. You're a professor, aren't you?"

An electric sizzle coursed through my bones, every muscle tensing with the moment. Anticipation exploded within me. She was the one. She would be mine tonight.

"Guilty as charged," I said, offering my most sincere smile. "Can I give you a ride home?"

A scowl crossed her face. Had I overplayed my hand? I had to be careful or I would lose for the second time.

"I'd like a ride. Thanks." She winked at me, and I knew then I mistook her scowl. It was directed at the girl behind me. Amber's head followed the girl out the door.

I carefully led her across the dimly-lit parking lot, toward my Dodge Charger. Not a practical car, but I earned it after getting hired at the university. My wife didn't like it, saying I should've gotten some small SUV to help ferry our children around, but we already had a Sedona for that.

My head was on a swivel as I directed her toward my car. Faculty might see us and report our relationship to my superior, but this was no relationship. She would never see daylight again.

Safe from prying eyes, I opened the door and she slid in, offering me a sly smile as she did.

I got in and started the car, letting it warm up a bit. The chill of the night was evident by the protruding peaks on her chest I couldn't help noticing when she slowly pulled the seatbelt closed. I couldn't let her beauty distract me from my ultimate goal. I did that once, and it nearly cost me.

"Where to? Are you at the dorms or do you live off campus?"

She shuffled her small black purse around, and the rose scent drifted toward me again. "I've got an apartment on Mill Street. The Kincaid Apartments?"

I knew the place and nodded. "Sounds good."

"How do you like school?" I asked as we got started. I offered my "concerned about you" voice I used when students were struggling in class.

"Just working on my generals, so... kinda sucks."

I understood her sentiment. She would never get a chance to discover her passion like I did. It was in college when I realized how wonderful it was to take a life.

We kept talking, and within ten minutes, we sat parked in the lot in front of her building.

"Thanks for the ride. I worried at first you might be a creep, but you turned out to be a nice guy. I appreciate that." She leaned over and gave me a kiss on the cheek, a spark of electricity arcing from her soft, warm lips.

My heart raced. Visions of what I would do with her played across my mind.

She unbuckled her seat belt and got out.

I watched her ass sway as she entered the building. After she disappeared within the doors, I realized she left her purse on the floorboard. I couldn't believe my luck! She must have been so drunk she forgot it. I turned the car off, snatched the purse, and ran after her.

The door was locked, and I had no idea which apartment number she was. I thought I saw her ascend the stairs, so I tried the 200s, randomly pushing buttons until someone buzzed me in.

Two girls walked down the stairs.

"Hey, do you know Amber? She left this and I need to return it."

"Are you her dad?" one of the girls asked. They both giggled.

"Or her Uber?" the second girl asked.

"Uber. Do you know what apartment is hers?"

The first girl smiled. "Two thirteen."

"Thank you." I raced up the stairs and heard a door close the moment I stepped onto the floor. I wondered if it was her.

I straightened my black shirt, smoothed it out, and knocked.

A moment later, the door swung open and Amber stood before me with nothing on but her sweater. "I hoped you'd get the hint," she said.

"All you had to do was ask. I like to get to the point."

"Then come in. Let me show you what I want."

I entered the apartment. It was small, with basic furniture and a computer on a dark-brown desk. Posters of old Universal horror movies decorated the walls. It felt right, like I decorated it myself.

My wife chided me for my fascination with old monster movies. I always loved them, since I was a child. There was nothing better than watching Bela Lugosi or Boris Karloff late at night with a bowl of popcorn and a soda. I still watched them, but only after my wife went to bed. It wasn't worth the hassle.

Amber went to the bathroom and came back with her hand behind her back. "I've got a surprise for you," she said, licking her luscious lips.

Not like the one I have for you, I thought.

She pulled her hand free, revealing a red satin ribbon close to three-feet long. She had my attention.

"For your hands. I like to role play," she said.

Bringing me an object with which I fully intended on subduing her with carried a sense of irony. When the authorities investigated her death afterward, they would have a hard time figuring out where I had gotten the binding, no doubt never thinking it was she who brought it.

I raised an eyebrow. "Quick and to the point. I appreciate that. More women would enjoy life if they gave in to their cravings rather than hide them."

"Sin is still sin," Amber said. "We all pay a price for it."

These were odd words from someone holding a binding intended for unusual sexual practices with a married man. The youth of today reveled in conflict, though I wasn't much different, if I was being honest with myself.

"I agree," I said, playing her game. The trick was to disarm my victim with charm. The moment they relaxed, I pounced like a vicious predator which I supposed I was. Vicious, that was.

She nodded toward the bed, and I took the hint, striding across the worn gold carpet and taking a seat on the black comforter. Unlike many young women I met, she didn't adorn her bed with endless pillows or stuffed animals. Two pillows, nothing more. I admired her spartan decor.

"Want a drink?" she asked, swaying a bit in front of me. I thought how easy the next few moments would be as she seemed completely focused on the sexual experience and not my real intentions. However, I also wondered how far I could take this encounter.

Typically, I didn't engage my victim sexually. Those moments offered too many opportunities to leave evidence. Besides, sexual violence toward women did nothing for me. It was an abhorrent abuse of male privilege.

But the way her ass swayed when she entered the apartment building set something afire within me. My wife had refused my advances of late, and I craved release. My hand only did so much to alleviate the built-up tension. Tonight might be the time I broke from the mold, mutually agreed to, of course.

The more I thought about it, the more anxious I grew. I felt especially wicked, contemplating how I would take her and how I would carve her body later. She would be my masterpiece.

"No thank you, I've had plenty this evening," I said, breaking from my thoughts.

She shrugged. "Fine by me."

Amber giggled then pulled off her top, revealing a black lacy bra covering her young, firm breasts, not too large but slightly larger for her thin frame. Her taut stomach reminded me of my wife when she was younger. Not that she was unattractive in her late thirties, but like all of us at that age, she had added a few pounds.

"You're gorgeous," I whispered. I meant it. She would be my pinnacle, my Sistine Chapel, my piece de resistance.

She playfully spun around. A black G-string held together with a gold clasp split her firm ass. She gave a little shake, and I felt my excitement grow. Was she giving me a sign?

I always wanted to try the forbidden pleasure of anal sex, but my dear wife refused on the grounds of it being a perverse and unholy act. Maybe with Amber I would finally get that chance.

"Have you ever tried anal?" I asked bluntly. If she refused, it wouldn't be the end of things. I had nothing to lose.

She turned back to me with a wicked smile. "Tried it? I prefer it."

Her words set my desire on fire. I needed her. My entire being yearned for her. I would take her not only from behind, but eventually, I would take all of her like I had with many before. She had no idea how ready I was.

Control yourself. Don't lose sight of what you really want from her, I scolded myself.

"I'd love to, but you must let me tie you up first. We both get what we want. Deal?" she said.

My smile couldn't have been more permanent. "Deal."

I pulled off my clothes and stood completely naked, my slightly-bulging belly a source of some self-consciousness on my part, but she didn't seem to mind. She nodded toward my hands, and I extended my arms for her to do as she willed. All I could think about was penetrating her. And what I would do after.

She straddled my chest as she leaned over my head to tie me up. A large nipple escaped her bra and grazed my lips. She tasted sweet.

When she was done, she smiled at me and licked her dark-red lips. "Perfect," she purred. I was ready for whatever she intended.

She slid off me, then pulled off her bra and panties. Dark areolas surrounded her large, thick nipples. She was shaven, and a slight-pink hue ran along her vulva. From the table next to the bed, she pulled out lubrication and something else I thought was a vibrator or dildo, but she moved so fast I wasn't sure. She squeezed a large amount of lube in her hands, then stroked my erect cock with it. She did the same to her ass until it glistened.

"I hope you enjoy this as much as I do," she said. She wiped her hands on the bed next to me and climbed back atop, hovering above my erect member. My heart raced, the impending pleasure teasing me.

Slowly, she slid down, with me inside her. The tight sensation was mesmerizing. I closed my eyes and pulled on the straps, unable to wrap my arms around her. I wanted desperately to be fully in her ass, to finish and then do what really excited me.

When I opened my eyes, I gasped.

"Amber?"

She pulled a rusted pocketknife from the table next to the lube and held it open, with the tip pointed at me. She turned it to the side, and I noticed the initials BR engraved on the handle.

"Sin must be dealt with. I must be cleansed," she said. Her tone changed dramatically from the honey sweetness of moments ago to a stern, commanding voice.

I nervously smiled, hoping to disarm her with my charm. "My dear, our union tonight shall cleanse us both. You promised me something. I'll be quite upset if I don't get it." I had many victims attempt to act tough moments before I carved flesh from their bones. None had the fortitude I possessed, and despite Amber's odd behavior, nothing gave me reason to believe she did, either.

"The soul is a delicate thing. Do you know where it lives?" she asked, pointing the dull blade at my face.

Jokingly, I answered, "I don't know where it lives, but I do know the eyes are the window to the soul. Perhaps you can see it from there?" I opened my eyes wider, trying to lighten the mood.

Though I was still inside her, my lust for her began to fade. I thought I might not get the chance to fully indulge in my dark longing after all but would get straight to the more pressing matter of killing her.

When she tied my hands to the bedpost, I balled them into fists, making my muscles tight and increasing the size of my wrist. It was an old trick I discovered when reading about Harry Houdini, while in college. He used to puff himself up and flex his muscles so when his assistant shackled him to whatever device he wanted to escape from, he had just enough wiggle room to break free. I let my hands relax and felt a slight give in the bindings. I grinned, knowing freedom was at hand, so to speak.

Amber shifted on top of me in such a way that my still partially-erect penis bent backward, and I screamed in agony. I knew it wasn't made of bone, but if it were, she would've broken it in two. I tried to rip my hands free, but the sudden shock of what she did made my muscles tense. If I was to get free, I had to relax, which at the moment seemed far from possible.

"I told you, a soul needs cleansing. And if you cry out like that again, it will be the last thing you do," she said in that stern voice, leaning over me with her chest lightly smashed against my own.

"What do you want?" I asked, for the first time feeling as though I would also fail to do what I originally came here for. And this, I scolded myself, was why you didn't engage with your victims sexually.

She pulled off me then, my limp member flopping to the side.

"A girl doesn't share her secrets, especially not on the first date."

I steadied my breathing, focusing on my wrist and wondering why I had been so foolish. I cursed myself for indulging when I knew better. I swore to never let my focus slide again. When I was done with Amber, she would be an example of what my rage could do. There would be no inch of her apartment untouched by her blood. Bits of her flesh would be spread over everything.

I felt one of my hands slip, almost freed from her satin tie. She noticed it and lunged at my hand. She clutched it tightly and pulled the satin bind until it dug into me.

"I told you," she growled when she finished, "the soul, your soul, needs cleansing. There are none who are pure. Not even me."

She waved the rusty blade in front of my face. It wasn't sharp enough to severely injure me, and I wondered what she intended on doing. Laying the tip of the blade on my nose, she ran it slowly down my face and chest until she closed in on my penis, still wet with lube.

"What are you doing?" I asked, growing fearful she might try something stupid. "Why don't we forget all about tonight and go our own ways?" Whatever it took to distract her until I figured out how to free myself was my thought. The way she lasciviously eyed my cock worried me. The longer this went on, the more I determined she would pay dearly once I was free.

"Have I told you about my grandfather?" she said, pulling the knife away and allowing me a brief respite. "He was a deeply religious man. Communed with God too. He taught me many things. He still does, even though he's no longer with us."

"I appreciate a good story, but could you do so without my hands tied? I've lost my desire to continue what we started."

She let out a giggle, licking her lips. "You know what my grandfather said about men like you? He said you were the scourge of the earth. Spoilers of virgins and desecraters of all that is holy."

If you only knew about me, I thought. *Your grandfather would roll over in his grave.*

My libido had faded at that point, replaced with a scorching anger. I would make her suffer worse than any before. She would pray for Hell as a rescue from my wrath. Her grandfather be damned.

"If you're so worried about your soul, why are you naked and why did you think having sex with a married man was a good idea?" I decided to try changing my tactics. Maybe if I angered her enough, she would make a mistake I could take advantage of.

"I'm a sinful creature. I regret my decision. I did think we could enjoy each other, but you kinda made that impossible. All I could think of was your wife. Do you have children? What's that make me? I'm no homewrecker."

I laughed out loud at her absurd logic.

She climbed atop me and sat on my chest, narrowing her eyes and pointing the knife at my face.

"You think this is funny? What I do is never funny, but it is necessary."

"Whatever you say. Just let me go and we can be done." The moment she freed my hands, I would inflict so much pain on her.

"You won't go free. Your soul needs cleansing."

"My soul needs–"

I lost the words as she gripped my head and pushed back, holding the knife to my eye. She brought it closer, the tip touching the outside corner.

"Your soul needs cleansing. I must be the one." Spit flew from her mouth and landed on my face.

I could hear blood rushing in my ears. My anger had grown fierce, and I trembled thinking about how brutal her death would be.

"Scared? You should be," she said, mistaking my shaking for fear and not the growing rage inside me.

She held the knife to my eye, the rusty blade moving slowly in my vision. One slip and it would pierce my eyeball. She grinned, bowed her head, then muttered a quick prayer. When she looked up, she plunged the knife between my eyeball and the socket.

A fierce, blinding pain shot through my head. I had never felt anything like the intrusion of the blade. I screamed in agony.

She cupped her hand over my mouth. "Shh. The neighbors will hear. Would you want that?"

What I wanted was the blade removed. What I wanted was to slice her body into a thousand pieces. What I wanted was to make her suffer.

Slowly, she pushed the knife farther into my head. Pressure increased from the metal tip as it wedged its way inside me. Its point felt like it pressed on my brain. I desperately needed to claw at the thing and pull it free. The hot, searing anguish raced through my head. It was the most horrific pain I had ever felt in my life.

"What are you doing?" I asked with a quivering voice, something I was used to from my victims, not from me.

"Your soul needs freedom."

With a focused determination, she moved the rusty blade in and out, slowly encircling the top of my eyeball. I could feel the blistering misery with each stroke of the blade. Despite the awful situation, I kept my screams in check. I didn't want the neighbors to hear, because once free, I intended on doing terrible things to Amber. No one injured me and got away with it.

I clamped my mouth shut. The knife sliced through nerves. In a terrible moment, my sight vanished, leaving me with one good eye. I breathed heavily, like a woman in labor, but I refused to cry out again. Her slow torture only made it worse for her when I escaped.

The rusty blade sliced through more nerves, and her breathing grew quick. Her chest heaved, and her red lips parted in a determined smile.

I felt something warm run down my face. Even with one good eye, it would be enough to see her squirm in torment when I finally broke free.

"Your soul is almost mine now," she whispered, her rapt attention to her work meaning she didn't notice my right hand wriggle free. She pushed with the knife, her tongue sticking out from her plump lips.

I braced myself like when a dentist drills into your teeth without lidocaine.

I struck her with my free hand, slamming against her arm. She cried out and ripped her hands free from my face. In my haste, I hadn't considered her reflexive action. When she yanked her hands free, she clutched the knife, and it sank deeper into my skull while pushing on the back of my eye, the orbital bone acting as a lever. I screamed.

A sickening, wet plop was followed by intense pain. It almost made me pass out. I noticed the eye she had been carving float above my face and land on my cheek with a sticky smack. I punched at her again and she fell off me, crashing to the floor.

I sat up, and my stolen eye rolled down my chest and landed on my crotch, staring up at me. Long strands of bloody nerves trailed behind it like a deformed octopus.

I howled and hyperventilated, the horror of the situation collapsing on me. Tearing at the other satin binding, I freed myself and carefully lifted my loose eye, wondering if I was destined to live with only one.

Amber regained her footing, pointing the knife at me.

"You've damaged your soul! Don't you dare do anything else to it," she snarled.

What the hell was I to do with my dismembered eye? A fierce anger swept over me, feeling a rage I hadn't succumbed to in nearly two decades, since before I learned to control myself.

Amber lunged at me, and instinctively I reached out to stop her, but that was a mistake. When I grasped her arm, my eye was still in my hand. The pressure of my grip burst what felt like a cherry tomato, the sound the most sickening thing I ever heard.

She screamed as though it were her eye smashed into bits of gore and blood on my hand.

"My soul!" she howled, backing away from me and gently touching the gory remnants on her arm. A streak of blood ran across her bare chest.

"You plucked out my eye," I growled, barely able to contain my rage.

She spat at me. "Your soul is beyond redemption."

My head felt woozy. Blood ran down my face. The room distorted and my brain fought to make sense of the new limited view afforded by my one good eye. The exposed nerves where my destroyed eye used to live fired several bursts of wicked pain throughout my skull. I wanted to repay her for what she did to me but didn't think I could find the strength to properly deal with her.

Grumbling to myself and pushing through the pain, I decided retreat was my only recourse. I hated to slink away like a beaten puppy, but it was for the best. I would find her later, once I recovered. She would wish she never met me.

Spit bubbled on Amber's lips. Tears ran down her cheeks. She mumbled about my soul and seemed distraught by the events unfolding.

That was my chance.

I backed away from her, picking my clothes off the floor, slipping into my pants and then my shirt. I couldn't accurately describe the level of pain shooting through my body when I pulled my shirt over my head. When the fabric brushed against the exposed nerves hanging from my empty eye socket, I thought for sure I would black out.

I stumbled as a shadow in my mind crept closer to consuming me. I fought with myself, determined to escape. The shadows receded and a rush of energy flowed through me.

Amber delicately touched the miasma on her arm, crying soft whimpers at her loss.

With her distracted, I contemplated carrying out what I originally intended on doing with her. But knowing my situation and realizing any soft breeze or light touch to my face would render me useless from the pain, I relented. She could blow a kiss my way, and the movement of air would light my nerves on fire.

I knew where she lived. I would be back. She would know the meaning of terror.

Fully dressed, I stared at her for a few moments. Still nude, her soft curves no longer elicited the response they did earlier. I saw her not as an object of desire, but as the vessel of my anger.

A jolt of pain struck my face, and I held back the scream I wanted to release.

"This is not over," I snarled.

My voice must have shaken her, and she looked up at me with bloodshot eyes and grinned. "No, it's not. I must have a soul."

I had enough. The wild look in her eyes warned me. She lunged with the knife held in front of her, and I stumbled backward.

She missed but scrambled on the carpet to reach me.

"I must have a soul! I need to cleanse!" She army crawled closer, and I stepped backward.

For a moment, I reconsidered leaving and wondered if I should stay and flay her alive. A little voice inside convinced me otherwise.

"You will die for this," I said. I bolted out the door, into the dimly lit hallway.

I stumbled down the stairs, my depth perception out of whack. Luckily, the girls from earlier had gone, and at this late hour, there were no other residents for me to avoid.

When I got to my car, I beat my fists on the steering wheel. Everything had gone wrong. I worried how I would explain a missing eye to my wife and daughters. I couldn't go home, not yet. I had to figure this out.

Peeling out of the parking lot, I screamed in the silence of my car. The heater kicked in, and the blowing air was torture on my exposed nerves. I cut the heat and drove.

I punched the roof of my car. The remains of my smashed eye on my hand created a sticky mess. Nothing went as planned. The urge to kill deepened within me. I stumbled upon a monster in Amber, and she needed to be dealt with. I could barely think as I drove, but one thought remained: revenge. My desires went unfulfilled, but they wouldn't stay that way. Amber would pay for what she did to me, pay with her flesh.

I drove for hours, trying to figure out how to explain my missing eye. The burning, throbbing sensation in my empty socket made it difficult to focus, though the one comfort I had was I was still alive.

Gritting my teeth while driving the backroads between Carbondale and Brownsville, a solution presented itself. I wouldn't need to tell my wife at all. She would never know about my deformity. My eyes were brown, an easy color to match. I just needed a donor.

Steeling my nerves and doing my best to ignore the agony consuming me, I went on the hunt. I would kill this night. Amber ignited my desire, and it would not be wasted. Fuck the pain. Forget everything else. I lost out on Jewel, then Amber. My string of failures was going to end.

Outside an all-night convenience store on the eastern edge of Brownsville, I spotted a perfect specimen. He was young, maybe a college student, but was thin and wiry. Pulling into the parking lot, my mouth salivated at the prospect of finally fulfilling my desires, and adrenaline coursed through me. I only hoped his eyes were brown. Shifting into park and cutting the engine, I stepped into the cool night with anticipation of the kill. It was due me.

"Hey, can we talk?" I asked.

When the young man turned to me, I smiled. His eyes were brown.

GHOST FACTORY

Harry sighed. Knowing he got nowhere with the teens, he slid into his portal and returned home to his cell in the Ghost Factory. It was the fifth time this week he had been laughed at, and Mr. Barrington's impatience with his failures was growing worse.

The routine had grown cold and stale for Harry—take the assigned job, travel through the approved portal, and scare the hell out of unsuspecting visitors to the haunted house. Lately, the living didn't seem as frightened. Engrossed in movies, books, and video games depicting far worse horrors than he created, they weren't afraid of curtains moving or cold chills. Even when he manifested himself as a gruesome specter, they laughed and pointed out how fake his shredded skin looked, as happened tonight.

The torn skin was, in fact, real. It was how Harry died at the hands of his wife, Mary, back in 1984. After he came home one night blasted out of his mind on heroin and reeking of perfume from an all-night flesh-fest, she flayed him in his sleep. When he awoke, he experienced a few minutes of absolutely horrific pain. Blood covered his body. It stained the sheets. When he tried to move, the sensation triggered electric jolts of agony. Moments later, he died. When aware of himself again, he was stuck in a softly-glowing green cell made of bars like a prison, but instead of metal, they were eerie green lines of light that hurt when he touched them.

Since then, he served at the whim of a man known only as Mr. Barrington. Harry, and others like him, were compelled to haunt houses all over the world. If they refused, Mr. Barrington tortured them with a green rod made of the same wicked substance as the cells they lived in.

When alone waiting for his next assignment, Harry thought of Mary and their daughter, Barb. He wanted desperately to find Mary and make her life miserable. Just once he wished Mr. Barrington sent him to her.

For his daughter, Barb, all he wanted was to see her again. After all this time, she would be an adult, and he longed to visit her, hoping she made something of her life. He didn't want her ending up like him.

All he had was the wrath of Mr. Barrington to face. The last haunting at David Court in southern Mississippi was a disaster.

The door of his cell opened, and the dark figure of Mr. Barrington entered. Over six-feet tall, muscular, and with jet-black hair and dark eyes, he would have been as imposing a figure in life as he was in death. Harry didn't know if the man was alive or dead, but he knew the man's temper.

"What's wrong with you, Harry?" Mr. Barrington asked. His gravelly voice sounded as though he had enjoyed decades of smoking.

"The kids just aren't afraid anymore."

"Bullshit. You know we run a top-notch operation here. Everyone else is doing their part." Mr. Barrington pointed his long finger at him. "You're the weak link here. Need another visit with the rod?"

Harry shook his head. "No, just time to think. Everything I've tried has failed. I can't relate anymore. Maybe...maybe if I could see my daughter, she'd inspire me." It wasn't the first time he made this request, though it had been a long time since he had. The last time ended with punishment from the rod.

Mr. Barrington laughed, then stopped when Harry's stern faced didn't change expression. "Wait, you're serious, aren't you?"

"I am. I want out. You know what," Harry said, floating closer to Mr. Barrington. A knot of courage worked its way through his corporeal body and gave him a spine he hadn't had in decades. "I won't do any more hauntings until I see her."

"You...refuse to work?" This time, Mr. Barrington nearly fell over from laughing so hard. When he collected himself, he stared deeply into Harry's eyes. The look was so cold that, if he wasn't dead already, Harry imagined it would've killed him.

"Tell you what. Somehow, you've grown some balls, and I respect that. Your next assignment...you'll see her."

Harry couldn't believe his little stunt worked!

"Are you serious? You know where she is?"

"I'll give you this one concession so you better perform." Mr. Barrington left, and Harry stewed on the conversation until the chime sounded, telling him it was time to leave and visit the world of the living.

Knowing this was his chance to see Barb, Harry composed himself and entered the portal. When he emerged on the other side, Harry immediately knew something was wrong.

A heavy-set woman in her fifties was tied to a bed with a gag in her mouth. The drab room was lit by a lamp on a nightstand.

Mr. Barrington stood next to the woman. He held a long knife in one hand, waving it gently in front of the scared woman's face.

She screamed through the gag, and he slapped her.

"Harry, it's about time you showed up. I thought you were ignoring me," Mr. Barrington said.

"Who's this?" Harry said, floating closer to the body. The woman's eyes reminded him of Mary.

"You know, don't you?"

"Barb?" Harry whispered.

"Ding, ding, ding! We've got ourselves a winner. See, Harry, I knew you were a smart ghost."

"What are you doing to her?"

"I don't take threats from the dead. You work for me. You do what I tell you. What we have here is motivation for you to up your game and scare the little shits assigned to you. Your performance lately has been terrible. You gave me this idea; don't look so surprised."

"How did I…" Harry's words failed him. Mr. Barrington was a monster. Was this how he compelled others within the Factory to do what they didn't want to do? He had only met one other ghost who relished the chance to torture the living. All the others were like him: trapped and coerced into their work.

"Stop trying to make sense of it. You're failing me, and I won't let that happen. Let's see what this does for you."

Mr. Barrington clutched Barb's left hand and, with her palm facing up, slid the knife from her wrist to her elbow, opening a long, angry line on her fair skin.

Barb screamed. Blood spilled out to either side of the gash.

"No, stop!" Harry yelled. Barb whipped her head at him, and she screamed. She pushed away from his side of the bed, more afraid of the ghost than the knife-wielding maniac.

"That's it. That's the reaction I want," Mr. Barrington said.

"Leave her alone. She's got no part in this," Harry said.

"Indeed, she does. She's my tool to get you back in shape. The world might not be as afraid of ghosts as it once was, but I have a quota to make, and without you performing, I'll have my ass handed to me by my boss. He isn't as gracious as I am. You will do what you're told, when I tell you, and nothing else. Am I clear?"

24

To emphasize his point, he ripped open Barb's white t-shirt, revealing her soft skin and ample breasts. If Harry had the ability to, he would've vomited at the sight of his nude daughter strapped to the bed. Mr. Barrington carved an X into her stomach. Barb howled when the red lines grew brighter as the blood flowed.

"Stop it! She's my daughter!"

Mr. Barrington looked across the body to him. "I know. Do what I tell you and she lives."

Harry floated back and forth across the room, moaning louder. His actions caught Barb's attention, and again she tried to push away from him and not the man carving into her flesh.

"Fine!" Harry said at last. He refused to look at his bleeding daughter and stared into Mr. Barrington's eyes. That's when the idea blossomed into his mind with a fury.

Possession.

He tried it before and failed terribly. When Mr. Barrington found out, he received three weeks of brutal torture from the rod. Possession was the escape route from this existence. Only one other had ever succeeded. Harry had spoken about it to others, but most kept their mouths shut out of fear of punishment.

Possession would allow him to end this.

Harry slammed into Mr. Barrington and was at first resisted, as though the man's flesh was made of the same green substance that kept him and the other spirits locked in eternal servitude. He pushed harder, while Mr. Barrington struggled to keep him out. They tumbled to the ground, where Harry landed on top of him.

"What the hell do you think you're doing?" Mr. Barrington growled.

Harry didn't say a word, focusing his energy on penetrating the body.

"You'll never get in. And then..." Mr. Barrington huffed, his strength fading against Harry's powerful push. "I'll kill her. I swear! I'll make it hurt so bad..."

Harry shoved his spirit into Mr. Barrington's mouth. There was no resistance. Harry channeled all his force into the man's throat. The warmth of the body consumed him. No longer cold and airy, he could feel muscles and bones, blood and flesh. Mr. Barrington's screams faded as Harry took control of his body.

The two became one, and Harry was in control.

Deep in the recesses of his mind, he heard Mr. Barrington howl. Harry grinned. Taking command of the man who imprisoned him felt wonderful.

Slowly rising to his feet, Harry gazed at Barb through Mr. Barrington's eyes. The disorienting view made him stumble. He hadn't been in the flesh for over forty years. It took a moment for him to get his bearings.

"Barb," he mumbled. She screamed yet again. He fumbled with the rope around her arms and feet, unable to get the fingers to work right. The knife Mr. Barrington used earlier lay on the bed. Carefully, he bent over and picked it up.

Turning back to Barb, her eyes widened. The blood continued to run down her stomach and arm.

He stepped closer, hoping to cut her free. Starting with her legs, he sliced through the ropes. With them free, she kicked wildly. He had to step aside to avoid her attack.

"Barb, it's me," he said. The words sounded odd coming from his mouth. He slit the rope around her bleeding arm. The moment he did, she smacked his head with a heavy fist. Unprepared for the blow, he fell to the floor and dropped the knife.

Barb twisted on the bed and ripped the gag free from her mouth.

"Who the hell are you?" she screamed. Before he answered, she grasped the knife and cut through her last binding. Standing over him, she quivered as she pointed the knife at him.

"I'm your father," he said.

She lashed at him with the knife and missed.

"Barb, please stop. It's me!"

Her mouth twisted and her eyes narrowed, then she lunged at him. The tip of the blade penetrated Mr. Barrington's shirt and plunged into his chest. The slip of cold steel penetrated Harry's flesh.

"No! I'm your father!" he cried.

The reaction inflamed Barb. She stabbed him several more times in the chest. Blood spilled from the wounds. Breathing grew difficult when she punctured his lungs.

For the second time in his existence, he felt life slip away, killed once by his wife, then by his daughter. Darkness consumed him. Again.

When Harry's eyes cleared, he didn't know what to think. Was he still in the flesh or was he somewhere else? The green cell emerged around him, bringing with it a sense of dread.

The door to the cell opened, and Mr. Barrington stepped in. One hand held the green rod. The other held tightly to Barb's head. He tossed it into the cell and laughed.

Harry howled as his daughter's head rolled toward him.

"That's it! Bring that anger to your work, and we'll have no more problems." Mr. Barrington left the cube and slammed the door shut behind him.

Harry picked up the head and gazed into Barb's eyes, sobbing. He knew then he would never leave. His fate was sealed, and Mr. Barrington would get what he wanted. Clutching Barb's head to his chest, he moaned until the chime sounded, calling him back to his work. There would be no more laughing this time. All of them would pay for what happened to his daughter. All of them.

KAPEROSA

RONALD AQUINO SAT IN HIS OVERSTUFFED GRAY RECLINER. A RELIC of the '80s, it was worn and haphazardly stitched back together on the arms and seat cushion. He imagined that when he took over the small house with his wife, Teresita, a few years ago, the previous owners left it because it was a piece of junk and they didn't want to deal with it.

But he convinced Teresita it should stay, a remembrance of the family before them. It was a weird way to honor the previous tenants, but he felt it was the right thing to do.

Teresita hated it. She never sat in the chair and refused to even touch it. Ronald didn't care. It was comfort. It was a connection to the past.

It was his connection to Teresita.

He desperately wanted a Red Horse beer, but nowhere near him sold it. He settled on Stag for no other reason than the icon on the can. It tasted like *yagit*, but he didn't bother to get something else. Not that it mattered much anymore. Nothing could drown out his sorrow.

Teresita. His heart. His soul.

She had been dead for three weeks, and the subsequent sadness consuming him had grown too much.

Ronald shifted in the chair and thought he smelled Teresita's perfume, a sweet lilac scent that triggered memories in his brain. He fought them, not wanting to revisit those painful recollections. What good would it do? She was dead. Teresita was never coming back.

Someone knocked on the door. Ronald sent up a prayer for the distraction from his memories. Slowly, he pushed himself out of the chair and shuffled across the room to the front door.

Teresita had never really loved the house. It was barely under 1,200 square feet, and she often complained it was like they were living on top of one another. When they both worked at home, it made for a cozy, if not cramped, workspace. But Ronald didn't care. He was near his *mahal*. Nothing meant more than that.

There was another knock on the door, this one more forceful. Ronald sighed and opened it without checking to see who it was.

"Son of a bitch," the short man said. It was his friend Blake. They had known each other from the moment Ronald moved to St. Louis three years ago.

"Look at you. Ron, are you doing ok? You look like Lou Diamond Phillips on a heroin bender," Blake said.

"Hey," he replied. They knew each other well enough that Ronald didn't have to say any more than that. He knew Blake would understand him.

"Can I come in?" Blake asked. Ronald stepped aside, and Blake entered the small living room.

"Smells like shit, man. Have you gotten out at all? Are you eating? You look rough."

Blake was never one to mince words, one of the traits Ronald found endearing, though at times it could be grating.

"What do you want?" he asked his friend in a monotone and emotionless voice.

"I'm worried about you. Ever since…ever since Teresita's passing, you've been distant. You need to be around friends. I want you to know I'm here if you need me."

Blake was a clinical psychologist specializing in family relationships. He started his own practice, and for over two years was the in-demand psychologist in University City on the western edge of St. Louis.

What Ronald didn't want was to share his most intimate thoughts with his friend, only to have it analyzed and scrutinized.

"I appreciate the concern," Ronald said in the same flat tone. "I can handle it." It was a lie, and he suspected his friend saw right through it, but he wasn't about to lay bare his raw emotions. Some things, no matter how painful, had to remain inside.

"Well, here," Blake said, shoving a six pack of Red Horse into his hands.

"Where'd you get this?" Ronald replied. A smile crept across his face and his eyes widened. It had been years since he had his favorite beer, and holding it lifted his spirits immediately.

"Don't worry about it. I know you need a boost. Look man, I mean what I said. If you need anything, and I mean anything, call me. You aren't alone, ok?"

Ronald looked at his friend. Grief, love, respect, sorrow…all of it mingled inside into a stew of emotions. The one thing he knew for certain was Blake would be there for him.

"Thank you. I mean it. Teresita was my everything, you know? It feels like when she died, my heart died with her. It's so empty." Ronald tapped his chest, indicating his heart. "It's like I died some that day too."

Blake placed his hand on Ronald's shoulder. "Grief is natural. When we have a bond as strong as you and Teresita had, it's very difficult to let go. She will always be part of you, and you don't need to deny that. It's ok to feel like you do, but please, don't let it control you."

Ronald didn't know what to say. He fidgeted with the gift of beer in his hands, and Blake seemed to take the hint, removing his hand from Ronald's shoulder and taking a step back.

"Hey, man, I need to get going. I wanted to bring you that," he nodded toward the beer, "and check up on you. Let me know if you need me for anything."

"Thanks again," Ronald said. He watched as Blake left the house, closing the door behind him.

TWO DAYS after Blake's visit, Ronald finally opened one of the cans of Red Horse. It was a Friday night, and his work week at the advertising agency was done. He had a weekend to do nothing, the kind of weekend he used to love when Teresita was alive. Since her passing, they felt empty and painful.

The first beer went down fast. He forgot just how much he missed living back in the Philippines. The beer transported him to his previous life, to a time before Teresita, to a time before the hurt.

The second and third beers buoyed that feeling and helped numb the dark edges. Never a heavy drinker, the slight buzz came on quickly but was welcomed. Ronald sat in the ratty chair and fixated on Teresita, wishing he could talk to her one last time. There was so much to tell her.

He sat in silence, replaying Teresita's last moments in his mind and allowing the grim situation to play out in exquisite detail.

Teresita was in bed, sleeping. The comforter was tucked under her chin, and her mouth was slightly agape. Her soft breathing matched Ronald's heartbeat. She was so beautiful. Her long black hair spread out on the pillow like a welcoming blanket.

Ronald leaned over and inhaled her musky scent, the aroma of their sex earlier in the evening still lingering. He stroked a strand of hair from her forehead, and her eye twitched but settled down. Ronald sighed, his heart breaking. It had to be done. She had to die.

Ronald pulled a six-inch knife from the nightstand, an old filet knife given to him by his father, before he left Davao, and one he had used many times.

"*Mahal kita*," he whispered, a moment before plunging the blade into her gently rising chest.

RONALD WAS AWAKENED by the sound of cans tumbling to the hardwood floor. Drool ran down his chin, and he wiped it with the back of his hand. His neck ached from how his head slumped to the side. The memory of Teresita he experienced the night before was still playing in his head, as though it was a movie on a loop. She, more than all the others, remained with him.

Standing up and feeling a powerful urge to piss, Ronald stumbled to the bathroom to relieve himself. When he was done, he washed up, splashing cold water on his face. Blake was right. He did look like a strung-out Lou Diamond Phillips. With his hands clinging to the sink, Ronald peered into his own eyes, searching for something, though he didn't know what. Truth? A soul? Regret?

After showering and getting dressed, Ronald grabbed the wooden cigar box his father gave him when he turned eighteen, by far the most precious object he owned. He took the box and drove to Forest Park, the largest urban park in St. Louis. He needed to get out of the house to think and be with his loves in a neutral setting. Strolling through the park was the perfect way to clear his mind. The beautiful spring day brought mild temperatures and blue skies filled with sunshine.

As he passed the fountain near the bottom of the hill in front of the art museum, he was overcome with a crushing sense of loss when he saw a woman and her two children playing with a kite on the lawn. The woman's long brown hair reminded him of Teresita, and even the woman's laugh sounded like Teresita's.

Ronald took a seat on a concrete bench to compose himself, resting his hands on the wooden box. Teresita was everything to him. The compulsion to take her life was not out of anger or hate, but of pure love. There was no greater expression of his feelings than to take the life of the ones he loved, and he got attached easily.

He opened the box, careful no one was around. Inside were dried hunks of muscle with a texture like beef jerky. They gave off a decrepit scent he inhaled deeply. It brought back a flood of memories.

There was Marianna, back home in the Philippines; Lisa, in San Francisco; Lydia, in Sacramento; Mary Beth, in Salt Lake City; Emily, in Tulsa; Megan, in Kansas City; Teresita, in St. Louis. Where else was his love going to take him?

Children's laughter sounded all around him. If there was one thing he thought he would enjoy the most in life, it would be to have children. He never got the chance because the compulsion to take the life of his loves superseded the opportunity. Maybe, just once, he could betray his urges and settle down long enough to have a child.

Staring at the dried hearts of the women he loved, he gently closed the lid on the box before someone noticed what was inside.

Ronald spent close to an hour on the concrete bench, watching the fountain splash and the children play. The warm sunshine helped lift his spirits, the antidote he needed to chase away the lingering darkness within his head.

He used the rest of the day to visit the art museum, pointing out the Monets and the exhibition on cubism as though taking someone on a tour, then finished his trip with a walk around the World's Fair Pavilion before hopping into his car and going home.

Once inside, the ratty old chair was moved slightly from where it once sat, the dust on the floor showing where it used to be, yet there was no trail from where someone moved it and no footprints to indicate someone was there. He narrowed his eyes, trying to figure it out.

How does that happen? he thought. He pondered the situation for a few moments but couldn't come up with any real answers. He put the box back in his bedroom, then shifted the chair back into place, making a note to vacuum sometime soon.

RONALD WAS AWAKENED that night when a powerful boom of thunder rattled his bedroom windows. He shot straight up in bed and was drenched in sweat, breathing in short, quick bursts.

"What the—" he asked out loud. He wiped his disheveled black hair from his moist forehead and took a deep, calming breath.

"Just a storm," he assured himself.

"Is that what you think?" a female voice whispered in his ear.

Ronald let out a yelp, whipping his head to the right, then the left, but no one was there. He covered his face with his hands and moaned softly. He wiped his face then opened his eyes wide. Lightning flashed outside, followed by another blast of thunder.

There's no way I'm getting back to sleep now.

Ronald climbed out of bed and first checked the box, then the clock. It was 2:37, way too early, especially on a Saturday morning.

When he was in the kitchen pouring himself a glass of water, thunder crackled again, rattling windows and shaking the dishes in the cabinet. He sipped the water and felt the cold liquid slide down his throat.

Thunder boomed again, but this time, a plate he left on the counter...moved. It shifted to his left by six inches, then stopped.

He slowly moved back from the counter. *How does thunder do that?* he thought. Shaking windows and rattling dishes was one thing, but moving something? That didn't happen.

The hairs on his arms stood on end as a sudden drop in temperature enveloped him.

Thunder crashed, and one of the cabinet doors flung open. A ceramic mug shot out, slamming against the opposite wall.

Ronald jumped back and clutched his chest, his heart hammering against his ribs.

"What the hell?" he shouted.

"That is where you belong," the female voice from earlier whispered in his ear.

He spun around expecting someone there, but he was alone. "*Churva,*" he mumbled, slowly stepping back from the kitchen. Whatever was going on there, he didn't want any part of it. Whether it was his mind creating fear from nothing or some weird, natural phenomenon making the dishes move, he wasn't sure. And the voice? It was ethereal and vaguely familiar, but that too had to have been something his stressed and fractured mind conjured up. All of that could stay there, for all he cared. He had to get out.

Rushing to the bedroom to get his clothes, more dishes crashed in the kitchen. Each broken plate and glass sent shivers down his spine. His mouth went dry, and his heart raced. Lightning flashed and thunder boomed, then his power went out.

"Oh fuck, not now," he said. He fumbled around on the table next to the bed for his phone. It was late, but calling Blake seemed like the right idea. If his mind was finally breaking, he trusted his friend to help set it straight.

"You will die," the female voice whispered in his ear.

He swore he felt a cold chill slip past his ear when she spoke. He spun around, but no one was there.

What is going on with me? Why am I hearing voices?

Then it dawned on him. The voice. It had been weeks since he heard it, but it had to be Teresita. He cursed himself for not recognizing it earlier, even with it slightly muted and ethereal.

If it was her voice, then his mind surely had shattered. He needed Blake's help.

He tapped on his friend's phone number, and it instantly went to voicemail. *Damn,* he thought. But what could he expect in the middle of the night? Blake had to be sleeping. Ronald called again but this time left a message.

"Hey, man, when you get this, please give me a call back. I want...I think we need to talk. Please." He ended the call and felt a knot growing in his stomach.

Lightning flashed again, but it wasn't as bright as before. The following thunder was muted and distant. But still his house was deathly silent with the power off.

Ronald clicked on the light from his phone and grabbed some clothes from his dresser. It might have been the middle of the night, but he couldn't stay there. Whatever was going on, he didn't want to deal with it anymore. Even if it was all in his head.

After slipping on his shoes, he grabbed his car keys and headed to the door. When he turned the knob, it wouldn't open. He scrunched his face and grabbed it again, this time with both hands, and turned. It was stuck. A frigid chill surrounded him, and it felt like ice was creeping up his spine.

"Come on, damn it," he growled, grasping the handle again, and with as much force as he could muster, tried to turn it open. It didn't even jiggle.

In his head, alarm bells sounded, a loud klaxon alerting him something was seriously wrong.

He headed to the back door, but it was just the same. He was trapped.

The lights flickered, and hope rose up inside him, though it wasn't like having electricity could help. Life just existed in the light; the darkness brought its own form of fear. But after flickering a few times, the lights remained off and he was stuck in the dark.

Ronald called Blake again. His call went straight to voicemail, and he clicked the phone off. He considered calling the police, but he always stayed far away from them. What if they asked to inspect the house? It was highly unlikely, but it was also dumb to invite the fox into the henhouse, something his *tatay* was fond of saying. There had to be something else he could do.

In the bedroom, he kept an aluminum baseball bat from when he played slow-pitch softball. He was never great at it, but his advertising firm played in a rec league and he felt duty-bound to play. They tucked him into right center field hoping better players to either side of him would help. He had gotten the wrong kind of bat and so kept it in his bedroom in case of break-ins. He grabbed it, and the special box, and headed to the back door.

At first he intended to smash the glass, but the door had six small windows separated by a wooden divider. It didn't seem like a great way to get out. He figured a window would work but was leery of breaking through. It would cost money he really didn't want to spend to fix it. Was he willing to do that just because he was scared? And scared of what? Voices made up by his own mind?

Ronald crept into the living room and sat in his chair, welcoming the form-fitted cushion from all his time spent in it. What was he afraid of? Broken dishes? That could have been from the storm. It had to be. What about the voices? They weren't real, so why was he afraid?

He spent several moments calming his fears by lifting the lid on the box and staring lovingly at the hearts inside by the glow of his phone, one of the hearts fresher than the rest. Maybe when morning came he would feel better. He checked his phone. It was 3:47. Hopefully the power would come back on soon, because coffee would've been good right about then.

Sitting in the darkness with his thoughts drifting wildly between Teresita, the Cardinals chances for the coming season, his parents back in Davao, and what he was going to have for breakfast, Ronald felt an icy chill along his arms. It sent goosebumps all along his flesh. He clutched the bat and held it close to his chest. It was an instinctual reaction, but no one was there.

"You will die, Ronald. Tonight," the wispy female voice whispered.

"Teresita?" he asked in a timid voice. He was greeted with soft laughter.

"You have more to fear than me," she replied.

He knew it! It was her, or at least his mind's version of her. She was dead. He killed her in the other room on the very mattress he was sleeping on before the storm awakened him. Her heart lay in the box on his lap.

"You aren't there," he said to the darkness, feeling ashamed of himself for speaking to the voice in his head.

"We are more real than you know," she replied. He had no idea where the voice came from. It was just…there. It sounded so much like Teresita, and it made his insides twist.

Something like a cold rope coiled around his arms and yanked them taut, pinning his arms to the chair. The bat fell and clattered on the wooden floor. Ronald screamed. The invisible bindings twisted around his chest, yanking him back to the chair. One of the unseen tendrils slid over his throat and pulled his head back.

"What are you doing?" he cried out. *How could this be real?* he thought. *This is impossible!*

Panic streaked through him like the lightning from earlier. It pulsed inside with every heartbeat. Maybe he ate something bad or was slipped a drug in his drink? He tried desperately to think of a logical reason why his mind was telling him he was strapped to his chair.

"I always hated that fucking thing," the voice said. If there was any doubt as to who his mind was pretending to be, that was all gone.

"What...are...you...talking...about?" he stammered. The coil around his throat made it difficult to speak as it slowly cut off his air.

While he struggled to breathe, a form appeared in the darkness in front of him. He thought it was another trick of his mind and was unsure it was there. But then a slight glow outlined a shadowy face. He watched as the shade morphed and transformed, the otherworldly glow illuminating the face until there was no doubt who he was staring at.

"Teresita?" he breathed.

Her flesh was charcoal and decayed, her eyes black as night. She hovered in the air, her hair flowing outward like she was underwater. She wore a white dress that swayed gently around her.

Ronald gasped, and the tendril around his neck tightened, cutting off his air.

She floated closer, and he could smell a stench of rot wafting from her. Chilled air circled his body.

"Surprised, my love?" she asked. He could only nod. "Imagine my shock," she said in an increasingly dark and powerful voice, "when you stabbed me with that fucking knife!" Her voice rang in his ears.

Had someone figured out what he did and was toying with him, bringing back his past to torture his soul?

The coil around his neck loosened, and his head drooped forward as he gasped for air.

"Teresita," he said, coughing and trying to collect himself, "is that really you?"

She rose up to her full height and towered over him. In life she was a few inches shorter than him, and he was only five-foot-seven. An ominous feeling settled on him. He wished and hoped this was only made up in his head, but the feeling in his gut told him otherwise.

On either side of her, more figures with the same slight glow appeared in the darkness, and all in similar white dresses. He watched in silent horror as they formed into people, into women.

"God no," he whispered.

Marianna from Manilla.

Lisa from San Francisco.

Lydia from Sacramento.

Mary Beth from Salt Lake City.

Emily from Tulsa.

Megan from Kansas City.

All were women he once loved, and all were women he killed to preserve that love. The panic that struck him earlier intensified, pulsating wildly.

"God?" Teresita asked. "No, there is no salvation for you."

"Where did you all come from?" he asked in a shaky voice.

"You murdered us!" Mary Beth cried out.

"All of us," Megan added.

"*Isa kang halimaw!*" Marianna snarled.

His eyes darted from one to the other, all women he thought would be the love of his life. All of them failed to live up to his unrealistic expectation.

Sweat ran down his forehead and leaked into his eyes. The salty sting made him blink several times, and when he did, all the women vanished, including Teresita.

He whipped his head back and forth, but they were gone. All

that remained was the coldness that arrived when Teresita showed herself.

"I gotta get the hell out of here," he said. Trick of the mind or not, there was no way he was staying another minute in the house.

Except, he couldn't move. His arms were still locked down and his torso was secured against the back of the chair. He struggled and strained, yet nothing moved.

He growled, then yelled out. His voice echoed in the silent house. "Teresita! Let me go!"

"I told you that tonight you will die," she replied from nowhere. He turned his head toward the voice, and her face was pressed against his, her frozen, rotting breath tumbling over his lips.

"You don't deserve to live," she snarled.

All the other women appeared around him, all of them so close he could feel their presence on his skin.

"No! No, no, no, no."

"You ignored me when I said the same thing," Lydia said.

"*Hindi na tayo maloloko*," Marianna added.

One by one, the spectral women plunged their terrible black nails into his chest, each one ripping through his shirt and peeling back a chunk of flesh. Ronald cried out. The invisible bond holding him to the chair refused to budge, and he was at their mercy.

"You said you loved me!" Emily screamed, then ripped off his left nipple. Blood sprayed from the wound as Ronald screamed.

"You said we'd be together forever," Lisa said, digging her nails into his chest and pulling free a handful of muscle and skin. The pain was so powerful that Ronald hit a falsetto with his scream.

"Do you understand now?" Teresita asked. "You lied to all of us. Your wicked ways brought this upon yourself. Death is coming." She clawed his face and tore open his cheek. Blood splashed his arm. The cold emanating from the women made his sensitive teeth cry out.

"You will never harm another woman again," Megan said. "Ever." She grabbed hold of his front teeth and twisted. A sickening crunch was followed by an intense shock of pain. Ronald screamed, and when he did, the air blew out of the ripped-open cheek and across the gaping hole in the front of his mouth where Megan ripped his teeth free.

The women took turns mutilating his body. Mary Beth dug her nails into his chest, breaking ribs and pulling them free. Lydia sliced his chest open all the way down to his slightly-bulging belly and pulled it apart. The searing pain of all those exposed nerves nearly made Ronald pass out.

"Not yet," Teresita said. "You cannot take the easy way out." She slapped him on his remaining cheek and jerked his head back. "We're almost done."

Each woman reached into his chest, all of them grabbing hold of his heart with a hand. The broken ribs from Mary Beth's attack created a perfect hole from which to reach it.

He could feel their cold hands on his beating heart and screamed. "Please, no!" he said, his voice growing weak. He had little left to fight them off with.

The women squeezed, and he felt his heart slowly stop beating because of the pressure applied. Teresita and the others yanked hard, and his heart burst from his chest, held in front of his face for him to see.

"Now you may die," Teresita said, taking the heart from the others and shoving it in his mouth. A taste of blood was the last thing Ronald experienced before his life left him for good.

THE NEXT MORNING, Blake tried calling his friend Ronald, but he didn't pick up. Fearing the worst after the cryptic message he left the night before, he went to his house. After knocking for a couple minutes, he tried the doorknob and it opened.

He stepped inside and was immediately hit with the stench of shit and blood; then he saw where it was coming from.

"Oh, no!" he said, sprinting across the room to the worn chair where his friend was seated. Or what was left of his friend. Ronald's desiccated body was split down the middle, from his throat to his belly button, and his heart was shoved in his mouth. The word Murderer was scribbled on his forehead in blood, which had since dried to a brownish color. On his lap was an open cigar box with what looked like hunks of dried meat.

Blake stumbled backward and nearly fell to the floor. He pulled out his phone to call 911, and a sudden chill came over him, as though the air conditioning had been turned on full blast. He turned away from his friend, disgusted and angry someone could do something so terrible to such a good man.

THE GOD'S EYE

DR. SAHANA BREDONIA RAN HER HAND ALONG THE ANDROID'S PALE skin, stretched taut over pliant muscles grown from stem cells implanted in pigs. Carbon-reinforced bone material supported the muscles, mimicking human definition: a perfect human replica. If only they could solve the synapse conundrum.

In theory, the synthetic neural network they devised should work, but synapses wouldn't fire on their own. Countless simulations said it was viable. So far, they had no success.

The simple solution was to implant a computer within the head for Dr. Bredonia's team to control the body. But simple didn't mean perfect. Computers constructed the illusion of life, but their team wanted more. They wanted to create life, not a false representation of it.

Advances in artificial intelligence over the past fifty years progressed the field to tremendous heights. Dr. Bredonia's team meant to push it further. Working in a sterile lab hidden within Dreamland in the Nevada desert, they skirted international treaties. Ethical or not, they sought to build a near-perfect android. They wanted to create life where life didn't exist. They

47

wanted to prove they were gods. The future of warfare, and possibly humanity, lay in their ability to bring life—conscience self-awareness—to creation.

They determined the best materials for the inner workings of the android. Everything they built mimicked the human body, but with enhanced characteristics. The carbon-reinforced skeleton behaved like bone yet stronger. Muscles were designed to resist atrophy. Even internal organs were streamlined, taking advantage of air, food, and water in ways human bodies couldn't. They achieved an astounding forty-five percent increase in bodily-function efficiency through engineered steps versus standard human bodies. But the synapse conundrum, getting the brain to control its own bodily functions, confounded them.

"I think we have it this time," Sahana said. Her voice was strong, with a slight Indian accent though she had been in the United States almost her entire life.

Her colleague, Dr. Stephen Parker, cracked a weak smile. He had heard that before. And probably would again. The solution remained elusive no matter what they tried.

"We'll see about that," Stephen said.

Sahana dedicated every waking moment to the project. Since her husband's murder four years ago, nothing mattered more than this. He had been mugged on a work trip in Los Angeles. According to the police, he fought back, but the muggers overwhelmed him and shot him in the chest, leaving him bleeding out on the street. The call from the LAPD was the most horrific moment of her life.

She held it together until after the funeral, when the crushing sorrow tormented her. More than once, bleak loneliness brought her close to taking her own life. Working on the project consumed her and became her only reason for being. If only they could solve their last problem.

Using 3D-modeling software, they combined the faces of the

five lead-project engineers, creating a composite facial structure. Gone were the days of only two parents. Sahana nicknamed the android "Bob" in a playful gesture soon after they constructed the face. Only Sahana and Stephen remained from that core team. The rest left a year ago when they recognized the project's imminent failure and lack of long-term prospects.

The facility at Dreamland remained staffed. Other military projects with higher success probabilities were well funded. They would occasionally borrow junior staff from those projects when they needed assistance or a break. It wasn't ideal, but Sahana and Stephen made it work. But their time was running short. More than once in the past few months their project was threatened with closure.

Sahana snapped the connector in place into Bob's right ear.

"Come on, you gotta work this time. You gotta!" Sahana said. She paced the room, biting her nails.

Stephen shook his head. "I don't see how this time is any different than the last. It's exactly the same program." The sides of his short brown hair were soaked with perspiration. He wasn't a heavy man, but the stress of the moment seemed to weigh on him.

"I've got a feeling. A hunch. Just indulge me, please."

"For the last time," he said, glaring at her. "After this, we're gonna need help. We'll need to bring in another team. We've been at it for over a year with no progress. Maybe the others were right to leave."

"Ready, Bob?" she asked.

"Could you please stop calling it Bob? You should never have given it that name. It weirds me out when you do that. You're giving the machine too much credit."

Sahana scowled but let it go. She would call it whatever the hell she wanted to call it…if it worked.

"Vitals are good," Sahana said, poring over the monitor. "Pulse is perfect. Breathing is stable. Oxygen saturation is adequate. We're good on this end."

It was the moment of truth. Stephen paused, his finger hovering above the mouse. With a click, he started the brain-regulating program that was supposed to give the android autonomous control.

The lights flickered.

"What's going on?" Stephen cried. He rushed to Bob and grasped the bed.

Sahana scanned the monitors. They blinked but showed positive readings. "Everything looks good. I'm not sure what that was."

The ground shook. The lights dimmed. A black shadow hovered over Bob. It expanded then contracted, forming a small swirling cone shape like a dust devil, with its tip centered on Bob's forehead. The shadow swirled, then forced itself into the android. Blue electric streaks sparked from the plug in Bob's ear.

An enormous crash like lightning slammed Stephen against the wall. Thunder boomed in the small lab, causing both scientists to cover their ears.

"What the hell was that?" Sahana shouted. "The system crashed. Are you all right? What about Bob?"

Stephen's body ached. The force of hitting the wall winded him, and he hunched over, gasping.

Sahana jumped from her seat, nearly knocking it over. She stumbled across the room.

Stephen held up a hand. "I'm...I'm ok. What about it?" he said, pointing toward Bob. "Is it ok?"

Sahana checked the connection to Bob's ear. Black soot covered the ear and cord. "I'm not sure. It looks bad. Something must've overloaded the circuits. I thought we were on our own closed connection. This can't happen!"

"Damn," Stephen said as he inspected the ear with Sahana. "Wow, look at the damage. No way we're gonna get that connection to work. We'll need to rebuild the housing. The internals are probably fried."

Sahana slammed her fist on the bed. "What the hell? This should've been impossible! Who knows how much work we just lost, how much time and money we've wasted because of this." Her voice grew quiet. "I can't lose this, not now. It's all I have left. Without it, I have nothing."

A vein pulsed on Stephen's forehead. "I know. It's not gonna be easy explaining this to—"

A low, deep groan interrupted him.

"What was that? Is that—" Sahana said as another groan escaped the android.

Bob's androgynous body twitched. His mouth cracked open.

Both scientists jumped back, startled.

"He's alive!" Sahana said. She raised her hand to her mouth, stifling a shout of joy.

"Bob! It worked! You're alive!" Stephen added.

Previous attempts had left their creation motionless and silent.

Stephen wrapped his arms around Sahana. "We did it! We solved the synapse problem! It's alive!" The two danced with joy. Sahana blushed when Stephen planted a kiss on her cheek, then gently pushed him away.

"We need to get it back to the observation room and monitor its vitals," Stephen said.

Outside the room, peering through the inch-thick, reinforced glass windows, two researchers from another project gathered when they heard the commotion inside. Expecting Sahana's and Stephen's disappointment once again, they found the two pumping their fists in the air instead.

"Did they do it?" a researcher named Ben Shelley asked.

"I think so. Look at the hand, it's moving!" Dr. Mary Stover replied.

"I can't believe it," Ben said. "Do you know what this means?"

The two stood in silent awe as they watched engineered life emerge in front of them.

Sahana called for help with the doors, and Dr. Shelley held them open as they carted Bob toward the observation room. Once inside, Stephen and Sahana connected monitors and ran a thorough scan on Bob.

"Looks normal to me," Sahana said.

Stephen's eyes glistened. All their work finally culminated in success. "This is unbelievable. We've been disappointed so many times before, I wasn't sure if we'd ever succeed. But look at it. It's alive."

"We've heard one sound, and the body hasn't shut itself off yet. We've succeeded far beyond what we've done before, but let's not get ahead of ourselves," Sahana said, tempering her emotions. "We've got a long way to go before it can be determined a true success."

Stephen deflated. Joy crept from his face.

"I'm just as excited as you, but we need to control ourselves. We don't even know what happened in there," Sahana said.

Several hours later, after Bob's extraneous activity ceased, the scientists left a couple borrowed researchers to watch over the android. They retired to their respective dorms to get much needed rest.

Sixteen hours after Bob's initial stirrings, something else happened.

One of the two borrowed junior researchers monitoring Bob woke Stephen and Sahana in the middle of the night with an emergency. Stephen heard yelling from down the corridor, near the observation room.

"Get me out of here! What are you people doing to me?"

Sahana crept behind Stephen. "What's that?" she asked, startling him.

"I'm not sure. Hurry, come on," he said. As they turned a corner and the observation room came into view, both scientists stopped.

"Damn you people, let me out of here! I need to save my wife! She's in terrible danger. Karina needs me."

Sahana gasped. Stephen staggered.

Inside the observation room, Bob paced like a trapped lion. Small spots of synthetic blood covered his body where he ripped out the probes. He lunged at the window, slamming his fists on it. "Let me out of here! I swear, I'll kill any of you that get in my way. I need to find my wife."

Stephen and Sahana couldn't tear their gaze from Bob as they approached the junior researchers in the small room attached to the observatory.

"How long has he—" Stephen started to ask.

"Almost an hour now, sir. He woke up, ripped out the cords, and began shouting. We woke you as soon as we secured the room. He keeps ranting about his wife," Howard Wolfrith, the more senior of the two researchers on duty, said.

"This is incredible," Sahana said.

"Why won't you listen to me? I need to get out of here and save my wife. They're gonna kill her!" Bob said, tossing a chair at the window. It bounced back, nearly striking him.

"How thick is this glass?" Sahana asked.

"Should be thick enough to withstand him," Howard replied.

Stephen clicked on the microphone to the room. "Bob, please settle down."

Bob stopped pacing.

All eyes went to the android.

"Who the hell is Bob?" the android asked.

"I understand you might be disoriented, but let me help ease you into this world," Stephen began. "Bob, can you tell me what's making you so upset?"

"Who's Bob? You idiots don't even know who I am? Get me out

of here!" Bob tossed a computer at the window, and a slight crack formed.

Sahana stumbled back and released a small scream.

"You, you're Bob," Stephen said, his voice shaking with excitement. "We created you. You're the first of a new kind of android, capable of marvelous—"

"Shut up! My name's not Bob! My wife is in danger, and you morons won't let me go," the android said, slamming his fists on the window.

Sahana grasped the microphone from Stephen. "What is your name?" she asked.

Her calm voice contrasted with Bob's anger. Her soothing tones had an immediate impact on the android as he hesitated his assault on the window. "My name is Adam Rinella. My wife is Karina Rinella. She's in serious danger. Can you help me?" He stepped closer to the window, and his facial expression changed. His brows lifted and his solid glass eyes opened wider. "Please, help me get out of here. Karina needs me."

Sahana raised a hand. "Let me see what I can do," she said in a quiet voice.

Bob nodded and his shoulders slumped. He turned from the window and quietly paced again.

"What have we done?" Stephen asked. "We need to turn it off. He's too dangerous. The power surge must've fried the system or altered the program."

"What's all this about a wife? The android couldn't have a wife or husband. They weren't created that way," Sahana said.

Howard pointed at the monitor, where he pulled up a story online. "Uhhh, you might want to see this."

The headline read "Man Murdered in Gang Hit."

"I searched the name our friend keeps yelling. Read it," Howard said.

Stephen and Sahana peered over Howard's shoulder, reading.

"No way," Sahana whispered, collapsing into a chair, "it's impossible."

"It can't be. Somehow, we downloaded the story by accident, implanting the memory, creating a false history. How else can we explain that?" Stephen said, waving a hand toward Bob.

"I don't think so, sir," Howard said. "The story wasn't posted until about three hours ago. And it's the only article I've found with his name," he said, nodding toward the android.

Bob glared at them. "Get. Me. Out. Now!" he said through tight lips. Anger leached into his face. "I have to find Karina." He beat on the window with his fists until the small spiderweb crack grew. Bob paused, running his finger across, then grabbed the chair inside, beating on the crack and making it larger.

"We need security down here, now!" Howard yelled.

Bob struck the window again, the crack spreading.

"Please, Bob, don't do this," Stephen said.

"My name is Adam!" he yelled. He paused, pointing at Stephen, and in a quiet voice said, "Call me Bob again and you'll be the first one I go after when I get out of here."

Sahana wrapped her arms around herself as Bob's menacing, dark glass eyes narrowed, gazing at her.

"This is my last warning. Get me out now before I make it worse for all of you. I don't know what kinda game you think you're playing, but it ends now." Rage built in his voice. "Karina needs me."

He clutched the chair and slammed it hard against the glass again. The crack he started earlier burst open. Glass sprayed on the scientists. Bob pushed the shattered glass and forced his body through the opening. Glass sliced and dug into his synthetic flesh, thin lines of blood emerging.

Stephen backed against the wall. Sahana clung to his arm. Howard and the other researcher, John Blackwater, pushed their way toward the door. They were blocked by two security guards brandishing tasers.

"Stop him, now!" Howard yelled, pointing toward Bob.

The security officers shot Bob with their tasers.

The electric jolts did nothing to him. He rushed toward them, then grabbed both men by their foreheads, slamming them into the wall. A sickening crunch as their skulls were crushed from the blow made Sahana cover her mouth to stifle a blood-curdling scream.

"Dear god, what have we done?" Stephen said. "We've created a monster!"

"You've created nothing," Bob said. "Stop babbling on about 'creating' me. It makes no freaking sense. I am me! I've always been me. I don't know how you dragged me here from Vegas. But I swear, if keeping me locked in caused harm to Karina, I'll kill all of you!" Bob tossed the dead guards to the other side of the room and ran down the corridor.

"Seal the facility! If he gets out, we're in serious trouble. We have to stop him!" Howard ordered.

John pulled a small red emergency lever, similar to a fire alarm, on the wall. When he did, a loud wailing siren screeched to life. The facility's emergency self-sealing procedure was set in motion. The outside doors locked. Each section in the facility closed itself to the rest. Wherever Bob made it to, he would be stuck there.

Howard keyed in a few passwords and silenced the alarms.

"What happened to him? There's so much anger. Was something corrupted in the transfer? What do we do?" Sahana asked, more to herself than anyone else.

"We destroy the android, that's what we do," Stephen replied. "I don't care how the problem started; our main concern now is to stop it from doing more harm."

He pointed toward the guards. "It should never have been able to kill any of us. That was directive number one since we started. I have no idea how it overrode that command. Right now, we don't have time to figure it out. It needs to be put down first, then we can argue over what went wrong."

"I agree," said Howard. "This thing needs to die."

"But what if we can capture him and talk to him? If we keep him secured where he can't harm anyone, maybe we can study and dissect the problem. It's much better if we study him 'alive' rather than dead," Sahana said.

Both men looked at her, mouths slightly open.

"No way, Sahana. I refuse to allow what we created to hurt anyone else," Stephen said.

Howard shook his head. "Dr. Parker is right. We need to stop it. Sorry, Dr. Bredonia, but we have to."

"But he's probably stuck in a room alone. He can't harm anyone if he's alone, right? We need to study him before we destroy him. We don't want to make the same mistake again," Sahana protested.

"I understand what you're saying, but we can't allow it to live. It's dangerous," Stephen said, gesturing toward the dead guards.

"Dr. Parker, it's in a lab. Look there," Howard said, pointing at a grainy monitor. "Looks like it's already hurt someone else."

A man in a blood-splattered white lab coat appeared on the screen. His head lay at an awkward angle. Two other scientists huddled together against a far wall.

"What's he doing?" Sahana asked.

Bob broke the leg off a chair and beat at the windows and locked metal security door. Dents soon covered the door, but so far, it looked like it was holding.

"Is there anyone else in there other than those two?" Stephen asked.

"I don't think so. I haven't seen anyone else. If there are, they're out of view of the camera," Howard replied.

The other scientists sat and watched the monitor carefully. If

Bob broke through, they would need to keep eyes on it and hope-fully alert whoever might be in its path.

Stephen leaned back in his chair, pinching the bridge of his nose.

Sahana sat with her head in her hands, watching Bob beat on the door.

"Howard, you got that article again? The one about Bob? Or Adam. Whatever its name is," Stephen said.

"Yeah, let me find it," he replied. A couple clicks and he motioned Stephen to the screen.

He began reading, stroking his chin. "Hmm..." he said.

"Hmm what?" Sahana asked. "We've already read this."

"I don't know. None of it makes sense. I hoped for a clue or... something," Stephen said.

"Like what?" she replied.

"A god's eye," John replied. As the other scientist on watch that night with Howard, he kept quiet most of the time.

"A what?" Stephen asked.

John closed his eyes. "A god's eye. Or if you prefer—a dream catcher. My grandmother made them all the time. Taught me too. It's an old Navajo tradition. Look," he said pulling up pictures of them on the monitor, "does this look familiar to you? Do you see the patterns? It looks exactly like what's in its head. I've been thinking about this for weeks now, ever since the last time I helped you."

Sahana gasped. "No..." she said in disbelief.

"Purely coincidence," Stephen said.

"Are you certain?" asked Howard.

John hesitated before speaking.

"What if we created a trap? What if—" he paused, tension filling the silence. "What if instead of creating sentience, we trapped another spirit?"

"What are you getting at? Are you saying a ghost? You and I

both know spirits or ghosts don't exist. There's never been any real evidence of it. I refuse to believe it," Sahana said, though her quivering tone betrayed her.

"John, that sounds too unreal, even for scientists like us whose career is spent working with projects bordering on science fiction," Stephen said.

"Spirit traps," John said, "just like the god's eye my grandmother made. What if, by chance, the neural networks you created acted like one of those? It's possible...right? You said this work borders on the bizarre. How can we discount this theory?"

"Sounds absurd to me," Howard said. "I don't buy your logic at all. It's much more likely they implanted Bob with corrupted code."

"I doubt it. They've taken months to build these neural networks. They're so intricate and weave in and around themselves like a god's eye." His dark eyes hinted at his seriousness.

"So, you're saying we accidentally created a spirit trap? And what we see there," Stephen said pointing at Adam, beating on the metal door, "is the spirit of Adam Rinella?"

Everyone stared at John. He sighed.

"Yes, I think Adam is telling the truth."

"Are you insane? That's impossible! Adam Rinella was murdered on the Strip. His head was found twenty feet from his body," Stephen countered.

"I can't be any crazier than Adam is right now. What if something happened?" John said as he fidgeted with the mouse, scrolling through image after image of god's eye's showing long lines of thread eerily similar to the neural networks designed for Bob's brain.

"It's not beyond the realm of possibility that when Adam was murdered, his enraged spirit refused to leave this plane, intent on finding his wife. And it somehow found its way inside our android, secured by the accidental trap you created."

"Yes, it's beyond belief, John," Sahana said. "There's no way what you propose is real. I can't believe it."

"Sorry, Dr. Bredonia, but evidence points me to that conclusion."

"We can't seriously consider this, can we?" she said, holding out her hands palms up, confusion on her face. Stephen and Howard looked deep in thought. "Oh, come on, really? You're buying into this?"

"I'm not a religious man, you know that Sahana. But John may be on to something. I mean, look at this god's eye and look at the neural network—almost identical," Stephen said, pulling up one of the schematics of Bob's brain.

"I know what we created, Stephen. It's not a spirit trap. We created electrical pathways, not a spirit prison."

John cut in. "Then how can we explain its behavior? How can we explain its actions? It's impossible for the AI to act independently within moments of activation."

"No!" Howard yelled. He pointed at the monitor. Two people lay dead against the wall in the lab. Adam stood above them, the metal chair leg dripping with blood.

"We need to do something fast. We're way beyond trying to catch it. We need to eliminate it," Stephen said.

Sahana opened her mouth to speak but stopped.

"Burn him," John said.

"What? What do you mean, burn him?" Stephen asked.

"Once a spirit is trapped, the trap must be burned. It releases the spirit back to where it belongs. My grandmother told us stories of her ancestors burning the god's eyes after trapping the spirit inside."

"Do it," Stephen ordered. "It's too dangerous. Whatever it is, burn it. We can deal with the consequences of destroying the experiment later. I'm sure our bosses won't like that we burned our work, but what choice do we have? I can't watch it kill another person."

"I don't want to get near him. Is there a way to activate the emergency incinerators in just that room? I'd rather not die in flames," John said.

"I think so, but it will take a few minutes to reroute the commands," Howard replied.

"Make it happen. But hurry," Stephen said.

Eerie silence hung over them except for the tapping on the keyboard. Each keystroke and mouse click echoed loudly.

"I need to try something," Sahana said. The other three scientists stared at her. "What? I want to talk to him before we incinerate him. I have to know. I've spent every moment since—" she paused, "of the past few years working on this project. It's been everything to me. I can't let it go this fast, not without trying to understand. Can you reverse the lock down procedure? At least so I can access the lab?"

"I'm not opening those doors! It can't be let out," Howard said.

"No, just the doors to let me get to that window," Sahana said, pointing at the large, reinforced window Adam had been trying to break since he killed the people in the lab.

"I don't think it's safe," Stephen said. "We can't risk another casualty."

"I know the risk. I'm prepared to deal with the consequences. Now, can you do it or not?"

"Yeah, I think so. But it's not safe," Howard said.

"I know. I'll be fine," Sahana replied.

A few clicks later, Howard said, "Ok, it's good to go. But don't provoke it. I don't know how much longer that glass can hold up."

Sahana nodded and raced toward the android. The rest watched her progress on the monitor. She stopped when she opened the last door between her and the window.

Cracks formed on the glass where Bob continued to strike it

with the chair leg. The metal-reinforced glass wasn't breaking easily. The android's efforts waned. The sound of the leg smashing against the glass slowed in rhythm when he saw Sahana. Then he stopped and stared at her.

"What do you want?" he growled. The glass muffled his angry voice.

"I want to know about you, Adam," she said, using the name he gave itself. "Why all this anger?"

"I told you, Karina's in danger and you idiots won't let me out. I have to save her."

"Yes, I understand that's what you think is happening. But can you tell me more about you? Like what happened to you yesterday? Can you remember anything about the attack?"

Adam held the chair leg in both hands, closing his eyes. "I was attacked on the Strip. We were about to go back to our hotel when four guys confronted us. They said something about payback, but I had no idea what they meant. I tried to reason with them. They struck Karina. I lost it." He closed his eyes tighter. "They grabbed her. They tore her blouse and groped her. I couldn't stand it. She's my wife! I had to protect her. So, I lunged at them. Next thing I know, they surrounded me. I heard Karina scream. I felt a blade at my throat—" he paused, looking up at Sahana. His glass eyes stared at her with an unsettling look.

"A blade," he said again, as if realizing for the first time what his recollection meant.

Sahana crossed her arms on her chest and felt a chill run through her.

Adam looked down at his body, the sexless shell created for their androids, and dropped the chair leg. It bounced on the tile floor. He stumbled back a couple steps. "It's not me," he said quietly. "This isn't me. Where am I?" He ran toward the window, slamming his hands against it. "What's happened to me? Where's Karina? I need to know she made it!"

If they had included the function, she thought tears would be running down its cheek.

"I don't know, Adam. We don't know anything about her. We do think you're..." she hesitated, unsure if what she was about to say would make sense or would enrage him further. "Adam, you died trying to protect your wife. We think we trapped your spirit inside that body. But soon you'll be free. And you'll be able to check on Karina."

A loud click behind Sahana made her jump. A loudspeaker at the back of the room came to life.

"Dr. Bredonia, I'm ready with the procedure," Howard's voice said. "You should be safe where you are; however, I'd feel better if you were back here with us."

She shook her head. "No, I need to stay with him. He shouldn't be alone." This would be the second time she lost something precious to her.

"Commencing in twenty seconds," Howard said.

Sahana stepped toward the window, placing her hand on it. Adam approached and placed his opposite hers. "Get ready, Adam. I'm not sure what's going to happen to you. I hope you'll be free."

"What do you mean?"

"We're setting you free."

"Five seconds," Howard called on the loudspeaker.

"Goodbye, Adam. I wish you well."

A loud emergency horn blared. Adam's eyes grew wide. He pulled back from the window, his head darting side to side. "What's that noise?" he cried. Then a series of clicks and the lab turned into an inferno, forcing Sahana to squint.

Adam screamed as the flames engulfed him. "What are you doing to me?" he shouted as his body caught fire. The synthetic flesh melted. Muscles charred. Sahana could feel the heat through the glass, but not enough to force her hand away.

"I'm so sorry, Adam. It had to be done. You'll be free."

Adam howled as flames incinerated his body, turning the engineered flesh to a dark-ashen color. Tables, chairs, and the other three bodies ignited. Bright, intense flames filled the lab. Adam's screams horrified Sahana.

She closed her eyes, fighting back tears. Her husband's voice echoed in her head.

Adam beat on the window. "Help me!" he cried.

One more giant blast of fire and Adam's semi-organic body combusted into a large pile of ash, leaving scattered pieces of carbon-reinforced skeleton littered on the floor.

Howard called over the intercom. "Shutting down the emergency containment procedure now." The incineration ended, leaving nothing but a scorched and silent room.

Sahana held her hand in place, the heat connecting her with Adam.

A sudden drop in temperature surrounded Sahana. Her skin felt icy. It was like being removed from the desert and dropped in frigid waters.

"Thank you," she heard in a whispered voice, "I'm free."

Then the chill vanished.

"Dr. Bredonia, are you alright?" Howard said over the speaker.

Yes, she thought, *I'm fine. I hope Karina is too. She shouldn't be alone. We aren't meant to be alone.*

Thoughts of her husband flooded her mind as she turned to leave and rejoin her team. She couldn't bring him back, but maybe setting Adam free would save Karina. Adam and Karina deserved a chance to reunite, even for one last goodbye. She hoped they weren't too late.

THE NIGHT I WAS BORN

The night I was born, the darkness hid. It peeled from the sky, retreating to depths unknown by man. My presence on this plane was not unexpected, but it surprised those awaiting my arrival.

Ancient Latin words preceded my coming. Forbidden strings of sentences, words paired in a perfect union of desire and fear, called me from the nether realms, my eternal home of torment.

Whipped from darkness, I was born—a demon to some, a savior to others. Hell to all.

The three teenaged girls within the circle of blood inscribed on cracked concrete in the basement of an old church screamed at me.

I opened my mouth to reply, and my scream forced them to scatter. I was bigger and faster.

The girl nearest me fell to the floor. Her frightened face and pained wailing when I feasted on her flesh enticed me further.

I warned them. They knew what to expect.

When I ripped her tender muscles and blood ran down my chin, her companions howled in fear. They attempted to flee.

Circling them, I corralled them within their bloody markings. I laughed. They were mine. As much as they thought I belonged to them, their feeble minds couldn't comprehend what I was or the power I represented. They never did, no matter how prepared they thought they were.

I ate heartily, none of the girls escaping that basement. New to that world, my sustenance needed replenishment.

Leaving the basement, I at first did not notice the little girl hidden within the baptistry. Too high on my feast of fresh blood, my attention remained on the fearful expressions I induced, my mind reveling in their pain.

I walked through the old church. It was dark outside, but my eyes needed no light to see. Forced to adapt over the centuries, they functioned well in the darkness.

The sanctuary was filled with splintered pews and fallen stained glass. Dust and dirt, caked from years of neglect, gave the place a sense of filth and decay I appreciated.

I stretched my large blood-red wings. It felt good to extend them after being confined in eternal torment and suddenly finding freedom. Blood dripped from my mouth onto the creaky wooden floor. I cared less about my presentation and manners and more about finding flesh to feast on.

I paused. I smelled her.

Chocolate and makeup. A pinch of fear.

I followed my nose, tracking the scent until I stalked to the bathtub they had used for baptisms. They knew the water did nothing, right?

I peered into the tall white tub stained with rust, and there she was. Dressed like a cowgirl, holding an orange, plastic pumpkin overflowing with candy, she must have been six or seven.

The little girl could barely see me in the darkness. If she had, she would've screamed at my appearance.

"Who are you?" she asked, waving her hands in front of her

face. "I want my mommy. My sister went downstairs and left me here."

I grinned. Her innocence made her blood smell intoxicating. To taste such young, delicate flesh was a prize so far unknown to me.

She cried, wiping at her face, smearing the red paint on her cheeks. Through her sniffles she composed herself, then handed me a piece of candy.

"Here, would you like a piece? It's got peanut butter. Mom says some people are allergic to it, but I don't think anyone can be allergic to peanuts."

She reminded me of someone from a past I forgot existed. Her offering suppressed my desire to consume her flesh. Inexplicably, I wanted nothing more from her. Not then. I couldn't fully explain why, but her innocent gesture rattled me.

"Not now, little one. Some day I will come back for it. I promise." She cringed; it had been decades since I spoke aloud into this world with my deep, gravelly voice.

"I want my mommy. I hope my sister is ok." She wrapped her arms around herself. "I'm Jewel. What's your name?"

"A name? My name? I have no such thing. I only exist."

It was partly true. I was once known as Zachariah. I had a family. A daughter. As a servant, I lost my identity long ago. I only lived to serve and be punished.

"That's weird. It's ok if you don't want to share. I get it. Mom said to be careful with strangers."

I growled, then turned from her. One day, I vowed I would find her. What would I do then? I had no idea. But at that moment, her innocence, which normally fueled my desire, repelled me.

The impression of a memory I couldn't unlock itched at my mind, and I grew angry with myself for failing to make the connection.

I would return. I would take from her when the moment came. Her innocence would shatter once she discovered the bloody mess

I left behind. Then, her fear would pull me to her. But at that moment?

"Goodbye, Jewel. We will meet again."

"No, please don't leave! My sister—"

I snarled and hissed, silencing her.

Stalking across the aisle toward the exit, I burst through the creaky doors, slamming them against the doorframe. I jumped to the air and flew from that old church, my senses overloaded by all the children outside dressed in costumes, screaming at me. A hunger rumbled within me. I was born once again into this world for a purpose, but until that purpose was revealed, a feast awaited, and I would let none of them trouble me like Jewel.

THE HOUSE ACROSS THE STREET

THE HOUSE ACROSS THE STREET SEEMED NORMAL ENOUGH, WITH faded-grey shingles and white-painted trim, cracked and peeling, exposing dark, weathered wood underneath. How often those slabs of wood, so innocently placed and carefully constructed, witnessed brutal horror within. Truly, if walls could talk, they would cry in sorrow and anguish.

The previous owner, a man I knew from high school named Ben Shulty, moved in about five years ago. He left our small town for the promise of something better in St. Louis. After an accident on the job left him hobbled and relying on a cane to stand upright, he moved back to live off the settlement he received from the dog bite, an injury probably far too common for postal workers.

Before I knew it was him, he caught me by surprise. He hobbled across the street when he saw me outside with my dog, Sarge, who barked at the stranger.

"How ya doing, Beth?" he greeted me.

"Ben? Ben, is that you? Great to see you! It's been, what, twenty years?" I said, shaking his hand. "Calm down, boy," I said to Sarge, tugging on his leash. "Sorry, Ben, you know how chihuahua's are."

Ben laughed and shrugged his shoulders. "Much bigger, and dangerous, beast did this," he said, holding up his cane. That was when he told me about his injury and reason for moving back. He had been going to physical therapy five days a week for months and hoped to get around without the cane soon.

"You want a beer?" I asked. I hadn't had anyone over in a long time. After my wife left me the year before, it was just Sarge and me.

Ben looked back at his house, then to me. "Nah, gotta get working on something in the basement. If it's not one thing, it's another with these old houses." We shook hands again, his left leg dragging as he crossed the street.

That evening, the first murder shocked our small town—a sweet, innocent fifteen-year-old girl named Anise Clover. She sang soprano in the high school's homecoming program and, from all accounts, brought the audience to tears with her angelic voice. She went missing around the time Ben moved in. Two weeks later, she was found in a field with her hands bound and throat slit, her blood drained from her emaciated body.

Two days later, I caught Ben lugging a heavy trash bag to the barrel by the alley behind his house.

Sarge barked. I picked him up and quieted him.

"Hey, Ben, you need help with that?" I called from the alley behind his house. I often walked Sarge there, avoiding other dogs. Ben struggled to move the bag, and with his disability, I thought he could use a hand.

He spun around, sweat dripping down his face despite the chilly autumn air. "Ah no, no, I'm ok. Thanks." He waved and returned to his chore.

I thought if the stubborn man wanted to struggle with the bag, that was his problem.

Later that evening, a report on the news of another missing girl caught my attention. Our small town of Brownsville rarely had serious crime. Two missing girls, one found dead and mutilated, were cause for concern. State police assisted the local police and sheriffs' departments. The missing girl was eighteen years old, an employee of Blue Moon Burgers, the local burger joint in town. I remembered her when they flashed her picture on the screen—Molly Willis. She had long blonde hair and green eyes. Dimples in her cheeks when she smiled conveyed innocence with a touch of seduction. It was shameful something awful happened to her.

I took Sarge out to clear his bladder and to clear my head of the evil within our midst after the news.

I noticed Ben dragging another bag to the trash barrel, and I crossed the street to talk.

"Shame about that girl, huh?" I asked, startling him.

He jumped.

Sarge barked until I held him.

"Girl? I don't understand," he replied as he struggled with the bag and finally hoisted it into the trash barrel.

"Did you watch the news? Girl from Blue Moon. Molly Willis, with the long blonde hair?"

Ben looked puzzled. "Oh, yeah. I did see that," he said. "Just terrible. I think she worked the counter the other day when I was there. Lovely girl. I didn't expect these heinous crimes when I moved back here."

"Trust me, this isn't normal for us. I can't remember a murder in years, other than the girl from a couple weeks back. Good thing we don't have daughters to look after," I said.

He smiled, a weak, forced smile. "Well, have a good evening," he said, dismissing me, running his hand through his thinning, peppered hair.

Sarge growled as Ben hobbled back to his house.

"Calm down boy, he's nothing to worry about," I said.

They found Molly's body in a field a mile out of town. A farmer stumbled on her while harvesting his corn, nearly running over her. I heard he almost had a heart attack when he discovered her bound and mutilated body drained of blood, just like Anise.

Our town was abuzz with activity. Law enforcement vehicles were everywhere. The brutal killings were the talk of the town. It seemed everyone was suspicious. The police were inundated with false leads, prompting a terse press conference from the sheriff, warning the public of wasting law enforcement time and resources.

Ben continued working on his basement, or at least I thought so. He carried heavy trash bags to the alley and refused my help whenever I offered.

"What do you think about all the concern around here? I'm worried about what's going on," I said. It was late October, and grey clouds coated the sky, choking out the sun. I held Sarge in my arms to prevent him from making a scene.

"It's not what I expected when I moved back, but I'm sure it'll be fine. Seems like we've got enough police searching for the bad guy. I'm certain they'll find whoever it is."

Sarge growled.

I held him tighter. "I hope so. I hate to see the innocent murdered like that. It's horrible."

Ben grunted and nodded his head. "Damn shame those girls got killed, that's for sure."

He paused.

"Well, gonna get back to work. There's never enough done. I'll catch you later."

As he walked toward his house, I noticed he wasn't limping as badly. He still used his cane, but I swear he didn't need to.

I was about to ask if his rehabilitation was working when Sarge squirmed and jumped from my arms. "Sarge, get back here!"

When Ben opened his back door, Sarge ran past him. I shot toward the door, hoping to grab him before he made a mess.

"What the—" Ben said when Sarge ran beneath his feet, almost tripping him.

I caught Ben at the door. "Sorry about this. Let me get him." Sarge raced to the basement door, barking and scratching it.

"Sarge! Get over here!" I nudged past Ben to get Sarge. He somehow opened the door to the basement. He was about to dart down the stairs when I scooped him up.

"Bad boy, Sarge! We don't do that." I closed the basement door, gripping Sarge tightly.

"I'm sorry, Ben. It won't happen again, I promise."

As I stood in the house, I smelled a faint odor. It reminded me of ground beef that had turned sour.

Ben's face was calm. He actually smiled. "No worries. I know how dogs can be. It's fine. Sooner or later, he'll come around to me."

I apologized for about ten minutes, scolding Sarge and trying to figure out what that smell was.

"Don't worry, he's ok with me. It's nothing." Ben tried to pet Sarge. My dog growled and bared his teeth, forcing Ben to give up his attempt at reconciliation.

We left, and once outside, I inhaled deeply, clearing my nostrils of that oppressive stink.

A week later, another girl went missing. She was a petite, red-haired, eighteen-year-old high school senior. Her name was Nicky Juarez.

I shuddered when they announced her disappearance on the news. How could this be happening again? With so many people looking for the evil bastard, I didn't think it possible.

Days later, they found her body with hands bound and throat slit, her blood drained. She had been shoved under the bridge on the east side of town, the busiest road in or out of Brownsville.

I bet I passed her body several times before it was discovered. It made me sick, knowing how close I was to the body, how close I was to death.

♦

"GEE, Ben, did you hear the latest?" I asked my neighbor. Sarge and I were on a walk through the neighborhood, and Ben again lugged a heavy bag to the trash can in the alley.

Sarge growled when we approached. I picked him up, wary he would dart off again.

"Hey, Beth," he said with a smile. Something about his appearance looked different. His hair? His movement? Maybe it was his complexion. I couldn't put my finger on it.

"Yeah, I heard. What a tragedy. Such a waste, if you ask me. Why destroy an innocent life like that? I tell ya, Beth, I hope they catch him soon."

I nodded in agreement. "I hope so too. All these pretty girls getting killed is terrible. The sick bastard needs to have his balls cut off. Better hope the police find him before the families of those girls do. I'd hate to be in his shoes."

Ben looked past me, as though focusing on a distant object, then snapped out of it.

"I agree. Better for him that way. It's just a matter of time, I suppose. Gotta get back to it. Talk to ya later." Ben's gait as he walked toward his house appeared different, better.

I called out, "Hey, looks like your physical therapy's working out."

He turned. "Seems like it. The program I'm on does wonders. Wonders! I feel like a new man. I'll be restored in no time! Soon, the monster's bite will be a distant memory."

Monster's bite? I stood with my head cocked to the side, unsure I heard him correctly.

Sarge growled the entire time we talked. I could feel him shiver in my arms. For some reason, Ben bothered him.

Several weeks passed without incident. The police presence returned to normal, and every conversation didn't start with "Did you hear about this girl?" or "Did you hear about that girl?" It was a relief to make it through Thanksgiving without another murder. But as soon as normalcy settled in, it happened again, during the first week of December.

Her name was LuAnn King, a fifteen-year-old freshman and self-professed nerd. She played video games and read comics, every teen boy's wet dream. When they found her, her long brunette curls were frozen from her blood. Like the others, she was bound, with her throat slit, her blood nearly drained. They discovered her body along the train tracks on the west side of town.

However, the killer was sloppy.

It snowed a couple days previous to her discovery, and the killer left prints in the snow. Small drops of blood formed a trail next to the prints leading to LuAnn. What caught the detective's attention was the pattern. The prints weren't evenly spaced. There was a slight drag across the snow from the left foot to its next step.

As if the killer had a limp.

In a desperate attempt to solve the murders, the police released these details to the public.

When I came home from work the day after the footprints were announced, I noticed Ben sprinkling salt on his sidewalk, the only clear sidewalk on his side of the street. What caught my attention was the way he walked. I don't know why I hadn't thought of it sooner.

His physical therapy had been working well enough he could move without a cane, but he still had a slight limp. When he walked, his left foot didn't go as high as his right. It glided above the pavement before setting down.

I watched from my front window across the street, my mouth hanging open. If anyone walked like the footprints indicated, it was Ben.

There was no way he was the murderer. How could he catch those girls? Every one of them could have easily outran him. He may have been peculiar but…murder? I watched and talked myself out of calling the police, my paranoia almost forcing me to make the call.

I scrutinized everyone after that. When I drove through downtown and got stuck at one of the three traffic lights, I would scan the sidewalks looking for anyone with a limp or strange gait. Man, woman, child…it didn't matter. I had to convince myself it wasn't Ben. If I could find at least one person that dragged their left foot and looked capable of carrying a body, I would clear my conscience.

But as the days lumbered on and the winds grew colder, my hopes dwindled.

I caught myself constantly watching the house across the street, waiting for Ben to reveal himself as the murderer. I stayed up at night, peering through the tiny opening in my blinds, expecting to see Ben with a body and relieved when nothing happened. I didn't want him to be the killer, but I couldn't stop myself. I even took a week's vacation from work to keep surveillance on him.

Three days into my vacation, I decided to find out more.

Ben had therapy every day at five in the afternoon. He never missed a session and left at precisely 4:35. I sat in front of the small window in my foyer, blinds drawn, peeking through a sliver of space. I waited as he pulled his Honda Civic out of his driveway, brakes squeaking, and drove away.

I opened the blinds farther to get a better view and make sure his car turned the corner. When the taillights disappeared, I made my move.

"Come on, Sarge, let's check it out." Sarge and I headed across the street under the cover of midwinter's dying light.

I walked Sarge along the alley behind Ben's house to first inspect his trash. I looked around, careful to keep a low profile. I paused before I lifted the lid to the bin. What if I found body parts? What if he left bloody clothes in there? I closed my eyes and raised the lid. Slowly, I opened them and peered inside at an empty container. He hadn't brought anything out. That meant I missed it, he hadn't finished what he was doing, or I was going crazy accusing my old high school friend of a series of unspeakable murders.

Sarge whimpered. "What is it boy?" I asked. He looked up at me with perked ears, then toward the house. He raised his nose, sniffing the air. "Let's find a way in," I said.

We approached the back door. I checked to either side of the house, but as far as I could tell, no one was watching. I knelt to look in the small basement window, but it was blacked out. I thought it odd, so we walked around the house, looking for a view inside, but every window was the same. I grabbed Sarge and went back to the door.

I had never broken into a house before and wasn't sure I should. What if I found nothing? How would I explain it to Ben? More worrisome, though, was what if I did find something?

I had to know. I had to clear my mind of the gnawing suspicion I had about Ben. Maybe I could stop him if he was the murderer.

I tried the knob on the off chance it was unlocked. It didn't turn. Several moments passed, then an idea occurred to me. There were six small glass windows that made up the back door. I could break through the one closest to the handle and unlock it from the inside. When Ben got home, I could tell him I heard a crash and chased off some kids that were throwing rocks. It was a weak plan, but at the moment, it was all I had. I needed to hurry before Ben was through with therapy. I had to be in and out of his house before 6:15. He would be home closer to 6:30, but I wanted to give myself time, just in case.

I found a rock big enough to break the glass and held it, poised, ready to smash the window. I paused. "Sarge, there's no turning back." He looked up at me and sniffed the air again. One last look around, then I broke the window pane. Shards of glass cascaded to the floor inside. I hit it again, making the hole larger, and reached in to unlock the door.

A putrid stench filled my nostrils when I entered Ben's house. It was like rotten, metallic meat. "Dear god," I said. Sarge wiggled in my arm, his snout darting back and forth. I shut the door behind me. My footsteps crunched on broken glass. I let Sarge down once past the glass, and he immediately ran to the basement door, scratching on it. "Hold on, let's look around here first." I didn't want any surprises.

I held Sarge's leash and forced him away from the door.

The house was lit by a light above the kitchen sink and a small lamp in the living room. The inside matched the decrepit exterior. Paint peeled from the walls. Brownish circles scattered across the ceiling. Black, melted candles stood in haphazard rows on the end tables. Olive-green shag carpet ran through the living room and back hallway. There were two bedrooms, both with the same dated carpeting. The small bathroom extended the theme with linoleum of varying circles and shades of green. There was no upstairs, only the basement. Once we cleared the first floor, it was time to check downstairs.

Sarge couldn't wait to get down there. He scratched at the door, trying to pry it open. I grasped the handle. If there was anything amiss in Ben's house, it had to be down there. I took a deep breath, inhaling the nauseating fumes, and opened the door.

The wretched stench grew intense. I forced down the contents of my stomach threatening to release from inside. Realizing the basement light couldn't be seen outside, I flipped on the switch.

Sarge ran down the steps, almost falling over in his desire to find the source of the foul odor.

"Sarge, get back here!" I called. He ignored me and disappeared into the basement.

I followed the worn steps down. Each footfall creaked. The smell grew more foul. I held my hand over my nose and mouth in a feeble attempt at filtering the disgusting scent. When I reached the concrete basement floor and turned toward Sarge, I couldn't hold back any longer and vomited all over.

Sarge found the body. Rather, he found the basin collecting her blood. He lapped the blood, gorging on the dark liquid.

A young girl, maybe sixteen or seventeen, slumped forward in a wooden chair. I had no idea who she was. Her hair was pulled back in a ponytail, and blood dripped from the slash in her neck to the basin on the floor. A large knife, its blade covered in blood, lay on her lap. Dried blood splattered the milky plastic sheeting covering the walls around her. An open trash bag sat next to her, more bloodied plastic sheeting poking out from the top. On the floor behind her, a strange demonic symbol was scrawled in blood. I thought I recognized letters, but I couldn't stare long; the horror was too much to view.

I didn't need to check if she was still alive. The full basin told me all I needed to know.

"Sarge, come here," I called. Over and over, I tried coaxing him away from the blood. He ignored my pleas, greedily devouring as much of the thick crimson liquid as possible. I was too afraid to approach the corpse to grab him. My legs were incapable of nearing the body.

How could Ben do such a thing? What kind of monster murdered young girls and collected their blood? And in this house in my neighborhood! My mind reeled at the gruesome discovery.

Suddenly, I heard the familiar squeaky brakes of Ben's car. Panic overwhelmed me. I pushed away my fear of the corpse and snatched Sarge from his feast, blood trailing from his mouth, and ran up the stairs. Just before I closed the door, I remembered to turn off the light.

I made it out the back door, stretched a shaky hand inside the broken window to lock it, and turned to find Ben staring at me.

My heart skipped a beat. I nearly dropped Sarge. My legs shook. I fought the urge to urinate.

"What are you doing here?" Ben asked. His voice was restrained calm, as if rage bubbled just below the surface.

I paused, speech eluding me. He seemed taller than before. Finally, I forced the word out.

"Kids."

"Huh?" he asked, tilting his head with his brows knitted.

"I heard a crash. We came over and found kids. Rock. They threw a rock," I lied. The sick, evil bastard terrorizing our community stared intently into my eyes.

"Why were you reaching in my door?"

"Ch-ch-checking to see if it was locked. I didn't want anyone to rob you."

Sarge's low growl gave me reason to cover his bloody snout.

"If you find anything wrong inside, let me know. I don't think they got in, but I'm not sure."

Ben paused, scanning the door and the yard around us. "Sure thing, Beth. Thanks for checking." He smiled, patted me on the shoulder, and unlocked his door. "Wanna come in for a drink?" he asked. He regained composure and lost the touch of anger I recognized moments before.

"No, no thanks. I better get going."

"Thanks again, Beth. I appreciate you looking out for me." A warm, welcoming smile flashed on his face.

I nearly sprinted across the street when he closed the door. Once inside my house, I locked the door behind me and dialed

911. In a shaky voice, I regurgitated all I saw to the unsuspecting operator on the other end of the line.

Ten minutes later, I heard sirens in the distance. Within moments, they blocked the street in front of my house. Blue and red flashes bounced off the houses. Officers in blue uniforms with drawn pistols advanced on Ben's house. There must've been a dozen or more at each entrance. The terror he inflicted on our town was at an end.

There was a loud knock at my door. Sarge barked. I grabbed him and answered the door.

"Ms. Wallace? Are you Beth Wallace?" the man asked. He wasn't in uniform but flashed a badge at me.

I nodded.

"I'm Detective Bishop. Did you call this in?"

I nodded again.

"Can I ask you a few questions?"

"Yeah, um, yeah, sure. Please, come in." I opened the door wider, when a uniformed officer came running toward us.

"Bishop," he said, "we found the body, but there's no one there. Seems like he left. Car's still there, but that's it."

"No! He was just there. I saw him!" I pushed past the two of them and ran to the street, shielding my eyes from the flashing lights and hoping, praying, I would see Ben.

I swore I thought I saw a slightly-limping figure several blocks away, moving farther and farther from the scene. At one point, he paused as if marveling at his work, then sprinted down a side street.

"He's over there!" I pointed. Two officers left the scene, chasing him.

They never found Ben. Disability or not, he eluded capture.

I didn't sleep for days after that night.

Detective Bishop returned to my house a couple of days later to ask me follow-up questions. Then he told me something else.

"Seems like he'd been performing some sort of blood ritual," he said.

"What?" I said, unsure I heard him correctly.

"He'd been using the blood of his victims to heal himself. Or try to, anyway. We found a notebook with detailed steps on what to do with the blood after collecting it from the girls—incantations, cultic imagery, and illegible notes scribbled on page after page. Something about reversing a bite from a demonic monster? I fear whatever it was, the healing worked. He got away."

I thought back to the improvement I noticed in Ben, how his limp had lessened and his cane became obsolete. I thought therapy had helped, but faced with this revelation, I wasn't so sure.

I half-listened to the rest of what Detective Bishop said. I couldn't shake the feeling I had been living across the street from a monster. Daily I walked my dog only feet away from torture. If only I had known earlier, I could've saved all those girls. I could've stopped him sooner. The guilt racked me for weeks after.

There weren't any more killings in Brownsville after that night. I searched online every day looking for a sign he was back to killing. Days turned to weeks. I never found reports of girls with their throats slashed, drained of blood.

About a year after Ben's disappearance, an elderly Asian couple moved into his house. I was stunned when they moved in, certain they would need to demolish that house of death. Somehow, it sold.

I wondered if they knew. I wondered if they knew about the evil that lived in the house across the street. Even at that time, when I walked my dog in front of that grey-shingled house, I sensed the terror it once held. I couldn't rid my mind of the basement, of that girl slumped over, and of Sarge lapping her blood.

THE ETERNAL GIFT

Ash Heidle curled around the corner of the brick building. Dark shadows danced in the alley ahead of him. The soft glow of the sulfuric streetlights didn't stretch across the entire street, leaving a swath of darkness like a barrier he shouldn't cross. Steam rose from the utility access covers in the streets.

He swallowed hard. It was then or never. He had sought these people for months. This was where they said to meet, a dead-end alley tucked between Olive and Locust Streets in downtown St. Louis. Originally, he assumed he read the message wrong, but no, that was the place. He was told a red door held his destiny. A bead of sweat ran down his forehead as he stared at the door.

It was time.

Shoving the growing alarm in his head to a dark place within, he straightened his thick winter coat and strode confidently toward the door.

Ash knocked three times as instructed, his knuckles stinging on the metal door. A small slit slid to the side, and dark eyes peered out at him.

"Name?" the gruff voice said.

"Heidle. Ah...Ash Heidle," he said, correcting himself. If done incorrectly, they warned him he would be turned away. That was the last thing he wanted.

The slider slammed closed, and a series of locks was unlocked and the door pulled inward. "Come in," the man said, though more like a butler greeting a distinguished guest.

When Ash accidentally stumbled onto the video game *Hell's Portal*, he followed what he assumed to be a joke through countless clicks, navigating their secretive website until he unlocked a portal granting him access to the Keeper of Hell himself. At least, that was what the guy called himself. Playing along, Ash soon found the guy charming and not as crazy as he originally assumed. The longer he chatted with him, the more he believed what he said was true: they found a gateway to Hell, and true immortality as the new King of Hell, was the ultimate prize. All he had to do was offer a sacrifice, open the portal, and...survive.

Stepping inside the red door, Ash's destiny awaited.

"Hurry in," the man at the door said. Standing about six-and-a-half-feet tall and nearly as wide, his hands looked as though they could crush boulders.

The entry hallway was dimly lit with a red bulb. The walls and floor were all red. Ash didn't know if he should laugh at the crude attempt to mimic hell or worry something terrible was soon to happen.

The man pushed past him and stalked down a hallway, turning back to Ash. "Come on, before His Darkness decides you aren't worthy of The Gift."

Ash followed, turning the corner behind the man.

Then reality set it. They entered a large room painted black. A single red lightbulb blazed overhead. Four women and one man in red robes, a black rope tied around their waists, stood on the other side of a metal table where a young woman was tied down with the same black rope.

She was nude and had a gag shoved in her mouth. Turning her head toward him, tears ran down her cheeks. She fought against her restraints and tried screaming through the gag, to no use.

"Ash?" the robed man said. He stepped away from the rest. His shaved head glowed red from the light. The man's dark eyes sent a chill down Ash's spine. His voice was calm.

"Welcome to the ceremony. You are ready, are you not?"

He stepped closer. Ash's heart thundered in his chest.

"I am," he replied. He had built up to this moment, practicing on small animals to the point he no longer cared to take a life. Staring at the girl on the table, he wondered if he could follow through with the ritual. It was the only way to enter Hell.

"I am The Keeper. Truly honored to finally meet you." The Keeper extended his hand, and Ash shook it.

"We have little time to wait. The Gift is ready. All you must do is claim it." The man pulled a large knife from his robe and handed it to him.

Ash inspected it—bone handled, with a six-inch blade sharpened so it glistened in the red light. It was what was to get him into the game.

The Keeper ushered him closer to the girl, whose eyes widened at the sight of the knife. She struggled against the bindings. The four women each took a position near her hands and feet as guardians against her escape.

On the far side of the room, Ash noticed a chair similar to what he had seen in beauty shops to dry hair, though the headpiece was far more menacing with cables and wires running down from it to the seat itself. He followed the path of a cable on the floor that ran to the table and up toward a drain. Not a cable, a pipe. It was where the blood flowed from the sacrifice to the system, unlocking his access.

"It is time," The Keeper said. Ash had wondered what it would feel like at this moment as he stood on the precipice of Hell. Thrilling. Exhilarating. Sickening. Still, he stepped forward. It was what he wanted.

Standing next to the girl, The Keeper chanted in Latin.

"Magister, obsecro noster accipere donum."

Sweat poured down Ash's back.

The Keeper continued the chant.

"Magister, obsecro noster accipere donum."

Veins bulged on the girl's neck.

"Magister, obsecro noster accipere donum."

Ash lowered himself, bringing the blade's edge to the soft skin along her belly. She screamed through the gag, but he could think of nothing other than entering Hell.

"Magister, obsecro noster accipere donum."

Slowly, Ash drew the blade across her stomach, a red line following behind it. The girl struggled, but the women made sure she was secure. Ash inserted his blade into her soft skin and dragged it through her flesh, opening another large gash. Blood poured down her waist and onto the metal table. A small stream flowed toward the drain. The process had begun.

The Keeper chanted. Ash, lost in his work, continued to cut the girl's flesh. He wondered how much blood he needed before the portal opened. He knew slicing her throat would give him the most blood the fastest but would also kill her quicker. The Keeper had instructed him to keep her alive as long as possible to gain the most amount of blood. It was what Ash practiced with all those animals.

The headpiece on the chair flickered briefly.

"Should I stop?" Ash asked.

"Continue. You don't have enough yet," The Keeper said.

The four women chanted the words of The Keeper.

"Magister, obsecro noster accipere donum."

Their delicate voices bolstered Ash. He gashed her fair skin. Streaks of red crossed her body. He saw her not as an object of sex but as the way to immortality.

The four women continued chanting softly. The headpiece flickered several times, as though an engine was trying to start.

"It is time," The Keeper said at last. "Finish the ceremony and enter your destiny."

Ash looked the girl in her eyes, her fear fully exposed. "Thank you for your gift," he whispered. Slicing the blade across her throat, more blood spilled out than all the cuts he made to that point. He stood back and watched the blood run toward the drain.

Across the room, the headpiece flickered wildly. Red and white flashes of light alternated like a wicked strobe light.

"Come, the time is now," The Keeper said.

Ash carefully set the knife down on the metal table.

The Keeper put a hand on his back and ushered him to the chair.

Ash wanted to cry. Overjoyed at his fortune, he turned to The Keeper. "Thank you," he breathed.

"You will be one of us soon. You have done well," The Keeper said. He tilted the headpiece back so Ash could get in the seat. Once settled in, The Keeper bent to look him in the eye. "I wish you strength through your ordeal," he said.

"Thank you for everything," Ash replied.

The Keeper lowered the headpiece.

Ash's heart pounded harder in his chest as a calming silence fell over him in the device's darkness. He breathed in slowly, trying to settle himself. Soon, his body was back under control.

A small pinpoint of red light appeared in the black void ahead. *There it is! I've made it*, he thought.

A moment of silence, calm and soothing, followed.

Then the light exploded, engulfing him in flames. The screams of thousands of dead souls surrounded him, each crying out for mercy. Horrific and painful, he could do nothing to stop their agony or protect himself from their cries. Screaming, howling, tortured souls called out to him.

The flames imploded and the screams abruptly stopped, their echoes lingering in his head.

"Welcome to Hell," a deep voice said, startling him. He turned to the left and realized he stood within a dark cavern illuminated by a reddish glow, though he could see no source for the light.

Standing next to him was a demon—red skin, black hair, charcoal eyes. The demon wore thick black pants but no shirt, his rippling muscles exposed for all to see.

"It worked," Ash muttered.

"Indeed, it has. Did you think otherwise?" the demon asked. His deep voice rumbled within Ash's chest.

When Ash bought into the realization he could take over Hell by beating what amounted to a video game, he leaped at the chance. He had played games his entire life. Why not find immortality within one? If nothing else, the virtual experience would be worth it, though not for the sacrifice.

"How do I start? What are the rules of the game?" he asked.

A grin slowly crept across the demon's face. "The rules? Hell has no rules."

"Sure you do. Every game has them."

"Of course. The sacrifice must come willingly. That is the only rule."

Ash thought about the girl, about her fearful expression, and wondered if she had voluntarily offered herself for his glory. He didn't know her at all. Why would she do such a thing?

The demon turned, and a path glowed red on the black ground. Without another word, the demon walked ahead.

Ash followed as the distant screams of the damned surrounded him. He would need to get used to this if he was to become the new King of Hell. With nothing left to live for at home, this was his only chance to live forever. The bone cancer he was dealing with was a torture no twenty-three-year-old man should endure. Fuck life. Fuck living. This was his reality.

They marched in silence for a long time until they crested a small hill overlooking a deep pit with a solid onyx obelisk in the center.

"There," the demon said, pointing at it. "It all happens there."

"Great, I wanna start my first quest."

The demon led him to the obelisk.

As they neared the sleek black stone, Ash noticed a metal clasp just above head height. "What's that for?" Ash asked.

"It's how this all begins," the demon said.

"How?"

"Place your hands through the ring, then all will be revealed."

Ash hesitated, fearful it was a trick of some sort.

"What happens if I don't?"

"Then you perish."

Going back to the living in that decrepit body wasn't appealing. Not existing anymore, not dealing with the pain...that was exquisite. But the lure of power called him. In this world, he could be something he never could before: relevant. That sealed it for him.

Turning his back to the obelisk, Ash placed his hands within the metal ring. The moment he did, flames erupted around the pit. The metal slammed tightly around his wrists, immobilizing him. He struggled against the binding, but it wouldn't let go.

"You better not lie to me!" he yelled to the demon.

"You expect to come to Hell and what...be given the keys? Your kind grow weaker and dumber."

Ash screamed, realizing maybe he made a mistake.

Behind the demon, a larger creature towered over him. It had the same red skin, black hair, and long black claws. It looked similar to the demon but deadlier.

"Master," the demon said to the newcomer. "The Keeper has offered another soul."

"What? No! I'm here to play a game!" Ash cried.

The larger demon stepped forward, the smaller demon sliding out of his way. He bent closer and snorted fire from his nostrils, singeing Ash's brown hair.

"Your soul is mine," he said. Ash thought this must be the Devil himself, the Morning Star, the Prince of Darkness.

The Devil placed a hand on Ash's forehead and he felt an immediate sensation of heat. When the Devil pulled his hand back, a small stream of black mist followed. Ash felt a surge of agony flow through him. It was like it had touched every nerve with pain and his body writhed against it. He howled and cried for his release, but the Devil did nothing to ease the pain.

Staring down at Ash, the Devil spoke. "The willing sacrifice. The soul now mine for eternal damnation. The gift freely given."

Then the Devil smiled. "I accept."

Flames raced up Ash's body. He screamed as they burned his flesh, searing into his muscles underneath and bursting his eyes in a momentous, cataclysmic explosion.

The pain subsided, and the blackness of blindness was replaced with the pit surrounding him. The Devil and the demon were gone. He fought with the binding, but it held firm.

The flames returned and eviscerated his body once more, until his eyes again burst. Blackness settled in, then the pit returned.

He had a moment to think he was stuck in a continuous loop, like a spawn-trap in a video game. The flames came back, torturing him all over again. He cried for mercy, but there was none. His world went black, then it started once more. The flames. The pain. The bursting.

In the distance, he heard the cries of the damned and knew his voice was added to that chorus. He dared to think he could find a shortcut to immortality and reign as the King of Hell.

Flames took him again, devouring his body and plunging him into darkness. The pit reemerged. He waited, hopeful the torture was over, then it started again. Over and over it went.

Ash cried out, the eternal gift offering an everlasting life.

FROM DUST TO DUST

ONE

HELEN CARTWRIGHT DUG her toes into the thick mud. It squished between them as she wriggled them farther into the muck. Her older sister Maggie sat next to her doing the same. Her parents were out in the lake with their three younger brothers, laughing and splashing. The sun beat down on them, blistering Helen's skin. She didn't mind. The sun felt glorious.

"What do you think this house is going to be like?" Helen asked.

"Momma said it was beautiful and that we would all have our own rooms," Maggie said. "Maybe we won't have to be gone for too long, though."

"I hope it's as good as Momma says. I didn't want to leave Kansas," Helen said, scrunching her toes and watching the mud squeeze through them.

Maggie sighed and leaned on her younger sister. At eleven and ten, Maggie and Helen were the closest in age among the five siblings, which meant they were often found playing together while leaving the others out. Besides, as the only girls, they had a lot more in common than their brothers.

Helen had doubts about moving to Appleton, Wisconsin. Growing up in the grasslands outside of Ulysses, Kansas, all she had ever known was the farm. She loved it there. Goats. Chickens. The barn cats were her favorite. Life was tough, but she enjoyed getting her hands in the dirt.

But the last few years, it had grown so dusty and scary. It got so bad that Daddy said they had to move. Maggie said it was because he lost the deed to the farm. Robert, their nine-year-old brother, said it was because the dust made the farm die. It didn't matter why; to Helen, they should have stayed put. God wouldn't punish them forever. Eventually he would make the dust stop.

"Are you two going to play in the mud all day or come in the water?" their mother asked. Beatrice Cartwright, who preferred to go by Bea, was a beautiful woman with curly auburn hair and dimples on her rosy cheeks. Maggie didn't think a more perfect woman existed. Fay Wray was pretty, but Momma was something more.

"Not right now, Momma," Helen said.

"I don't want fish nibbling on my toes," Maggie added.

Charlie, their seven-year-old brother, held their youngest sibling, three-year-old Henry, in his arms, bobbing up and down, making the younger boy shout and laugh. When Henry heard Maggie say something about the fish nibbling her toes, he changed his mind about the joy of splashing in the lake and turned from laughter to fear. He cried for Charlie to take him out, patting his head and pointing toward the sisters.

"Maggie!" their mother said. "Do you see what you've done to little Henry?"

Their father, Richard Cartwright, scowled at them, then turned to Henry. "Those fishes won't do nothing to you. Those piggies are safe. Maggie! Apologize to your brother."

Maggie sighed but didn't dare defy Daddy. "I'm sorry, Henry. Those fish won't hurt you. They only like the toes of little girls. You're not in any danger."

Henry looked to Charlie, then back at their mother.

"She's right," Bea said. "You have nothing to worry about."

Henry stopped fidgeting, and just like that, the mirth returned.

The two girls earned a stern look from their father, but he didn't say anything else.

Helen wasn't looking forward to the ten mile walk the family still had until they reached the house, but once there, they wouldn't have to leave. She leaned back and enjoyed the warm sunshine, closing her eyes and daydreaming about fields of daisies.

Two

HELEN'S HEART thumped in her chest. A small flickering flame illuminated the front window of the house. The stars and full moon overhead gave them enough light to see, but standing outside their new home in the middle of the night brought a sense of relief and a hint of trepidation.

The house was much larger than she expected. Her father must have had the same thoughts as he whistled loudly.

"Would you look at that?" he said. "Can you believe that we get to live here?"

Their mom sidled up next to him, placing her hand in his. Henry was asleep and draped over her shoulder, but she never complained about the extra weight.

"It's lovely," she whispered.

"Does this mean I get my own room?" her little brother Robert asked.

"Me too?" her other brother Charlie asked.

"All of you can have your very own bedroom," their daddy said. "Come, let's see if Mr. Argyle is there."

Helen heard the name before. When her father proposed they leave Kansas for Wisconsin, he told the family about Mr. Argyle, an old friend of his late father. He was a veteran of the Great War and fought in the Rhineland. She heard rumors trouble was stirring there again, and the German Chancellor, a man by the name of Adolf Hitler, was causing problems. She cared little for events on the other side of the world. What she cared about was what Mr. Argyle was doing for them.

"Let's get inside before the bugs eat us alive," her father said.

Helen wasn't sure how late it was. Her father once had a watch but sold it on their northern journey so they could eat.

If this Mr. Argyle was up, he must be a night owl.

They followed her daddy as he climbed the stone steps. He turned back to them, straightened his shirt, then knocked on the door.

In the quiet night, his knuckles on the solid wood sounded like it could wake the dead. Helen's heart pounded harder in her chest. What if they were at the wrong house? What if this Mr. Argyle was a bad person?

Someone shuffled inside. Helen, Robert, and Charlie all huddled closer to Maggie. The deadbolt slid free, and the door creaked open.

"Hello?" the man asked. He was tall and lean, with a hauntingly-gaunt face. Thin strands of black hair were plastered on his pale forehead. Thin red lips covered crooked teeth.

Helen thought she was looking at Nosferatu. She blinked her eyes and grabbed Maggie's arm, pulling herself closer.

"Mr. Argyle?" her father asked.

"Indeed I am. Are you Mr. Cartwright?"

"Yes, sir," her daddy said, "and my family."

"I see. Please, come in. I was expecting you days ago and thought you might have reconsidered the offer."

He held the door open and gently waved them in.

"No, sir. Travel took a bit longer than expected. We took the train as far as we could and have been on foot since."

Mr. Argyle raised an eyebrow. "Is that so? You'll be pleased to know we have a Model T available to you, assuming you know how to drive?"

"Of course, sir. Thank you kindly."

"Please, come into the parlor and we can discuss our arrangement. I know it's late, but it's best if we settle things now."

Helen gawked at a large grandfather clock ticking diligently at the end of the hall. It was ten thirty-five, much later than her normal bedtime.

They followed Mr. Argyle into the parlor, a room at the front of the house decorated with rich, dark mahogany wood and a deep-red velvet wallpaper with a Greek-motif pattern. A large, plush couch, dark brown like the surrounding wood, lined the wall close to the door. A flickering candle sat atop a small table in the front window.

"Children, don't touch anything," their mother said. "Be very careful."

"I assure you, Mrs. Cartwright, the children are more than welcome in here," Mr. Argyle said.

"Please, just call me Bea," she replied.

Mr. Argyle nodded in understanding, then crossed the room, turning around to address the assembled Cartwrights.

"It has been my greatest pleasure to offer you this opportunity to watch over Argyle Manor while I'm on my travels. Your father," he said to their daddy, "saved my life during the war. It is fitting that I return the favor."

"Not to sound disrespectful, but how did you know about our predicament?" her daddy asked.

Helen perked up. She had no idea how her daddy was connected with this man and assumed he knew about him before they were offered the opportunity to live there.

"A man of my means knows many things. I've been watching over you ever since your father passed. It was his dying wish that you be protected. Since I owed him a life debt—twice—it was the least I could do."

Her daddy seemed pleased with the answer, and Mr. Argyle continued.

"Argyle Manor is yours while I'm gone. There are no rooms off limits other than my personal quarters on the third floor. Under no circumstances should anyone venture up there. Otherwise, settle in and make it your home. The children," he said, eying each one of them in turn, "are welcome to run and play as much as they want. The woods at the back of the property are thick, and at night, wolves like to lurk among the trees. I'd be careful going there if I were you." He winked. The gesture made Helen shudder. There was something off about the man, something more than just an uncanny resemblance to the creature from the movie, but she couldn't figure it out.

"As I mentioned earlier, there's a Model T at your disposal. It's in the barn in the back. All I ask is for a ride to the train station in the morning."

"Of course, thank you," her daddy said.

"Now, I presume you all would like a good night's sleep. Let me show you the bedrooms, and you may choose which ones you want."

They followed Mr. Argyle out of the parlor and were led on a brief tour of the massive house. Helen was dismayed to find out she wouldn't have her own room but would have to share with her older sister. All three of her brothers had to share a room as well. That left her parents a room to themselves, which they hadn't had in their little farmhouse in Kansas. Even with the need to room with her sister, the accommodations were nicer than any she ever had.

Mr. Argyle showed them the stairs to the third floor but didn't take them up. "The third floor is where I've placed all my belongings while I'm gone. Though I did say the children had the run of the house, I'd prefer if no one disturbed my personal rooms. My bedroom is up here. I have many precious items I've collected over the years packed away as well, and it would be best if they were left undisturbed."

"You have my word that we will leave them alone," her father said. "There's plenty of house to enjoy without going up there."

"Much appreciated," Mr. Argyle said.

"You've seen the wash room and the rest of the house. I confess, I'm not much of a night person, and I'm ready to retire for the evening. Mr. Cartwright, I will need to be going by nine o'clock. Can we be ready by then?"

"Of course, sir."

"Good. Now, if you'll excuse me, I feel the call of my bed." Mr. Argyle left and slowly climbed the creaky stairs to the mysterious third floor.

In the morning, her daddy drove him to the train station.

THREE

OVER THE NEXT WEEK, the family settled into Argyle Manor easily enough. They hadn't brought many belongings with them other than a few changes of clothes. They didn't have much to begin with, and what they did have had to be left behind because they could only carry so much.

Helen's mom was busy sewing clothes for the children using the sewing room on the first floor. She discovered discounted bolts of fabric at a general store in town and convinced their daddy to part with the money.

Their daddy, along with her brothers Robert and Charlie, worked in a garden in the backyard. Mr. Argyle left a stocked pantry, but her daddy thought it best to prepare for the worst. Though he had a steady stream of income, his attitude had changed ever since the stock market crash in 1929. Helen didn't know much about what a stock market was—and still didn't—but she did know that when she was the same age as her youngest brother Henry, her daddy lost his job and they were suddenly poor because of events tied to what he called "the stock market."

The situation they were in wasn't much different, except there were more Cartwrights to look after.

Three weeks into their new life, Helen overheard her parents discussing what sounded like a very serious situation when she was trying to go to sleep. Her room was down the hall from theirs, but their voices carried. She and Maggie sat upright in their beds and listened intently, their eyes growing wider the more they heard.

"I can't believe the weather here is just as bad as Kansas," her daddy said.

"Dear, it's only been a few weeks. Surely it can't be that bad. Give it time," her mother replied.

"We should've seen something sprout by now."

"Maybe it takes things a little longer up here," she replied.

"I'm worried that we might be in a worse predicament than when we left. Sure, we have a stocked pantry now, but what happens when winter comes and we don't have anything to refill it? Having this nice house to live in is great, but it doesn't put food in the bellies of our children," her daddy said.

Helen and Maggie exchanged a worried glance.

"How long do you think we'll be here?" her mother asked.

"Mr. Argyle said it could be anywhere from a year to two years."

Her mother paused before replying. "As long as the money doesn't stop arriving, we can buy what we need."

"Bea, if we can't save anything, how are we going to live after Mr. Argyle comes back? We won't have a house. We'll be worse off than when we started. If we can't get these crops to grow, it could be disastrous for us."

"Then let's hope we have God's favor and things will turn around soon," she replied.

Their parents' door creaked open, and the girls hurried to cover themselves with a blanket, feigning sleep. Moments later, their door slowly opened a crack, then was gently closed.

Waiting a few moments, Helen whispered to her sister. "Do you think it's as bad as daddy says?"

"I hope not," Maggie replied. "Maybe we can do something to help."

"Like what?"

"I dunno, but I'm sure there's something we can do."

The girls fell silent, and Helen struggled to go to sleep as her mind continued to play her parents' conversation over and over in her head.

THE NEXT MORNING, Helen and Maggie sleepily shuffled to the dining room. Her mother had made oatmeal for the family. Her brothers were all seated at the table. Charlie was poking at Robert, and Henry fidgeted in his chair.

"O-meal, o-meal," the littlest Cartwright said.

"Shut up, Henry," Robert said.

"No. O-meal," he replied, sticking his tongue out. He then coughed. It had gotten worse ever since they moved in, and Helen wondered if maybe he caught some kind of bug, though it seemed to linger a long time.

Helen shook her head at her little brothers, especially as Robert's face turned as red as a beet. She could tell he was ready to snap at Henry, but when their daddy entered the room, Robert let his anger go.

"Children," he said by way of introduction, "good morning to you all."

"Morning, Daddy," Helen said, her siblings joining in.

"I'm going to need help in the garden again," he said to Robert and Charlie. "We need to make sure every weed is gone and that every seed we planted is watered. We'll have plenty of work to do."

Helen's brothers frowned.

Then their daddy turned to her and Maggie. "The two of you will need to help as well. The family is going to need it."

"But Daddy," Maggie whined.

He held up a hand. "I know that you've not spent much time working the land, but it's far past time that you and your sister got your hands dirty."

Helen crossed her arms over her chest and frowned, her bottom lip pushed out.

"Pouting will not do you any good," her daddy said. "After breakfast, change into some work clothes and meet us out back."

Helen slowly stuffed the oatmeal into her mouth as a way of protest. All she managed to do was make it cold by the time she was done.

After breakfast, Maggie and Helen headed out back to help their daddy and brothers work the garden. Their daddy turned to them; his face was bright red. Helen thought it was from the heat and humid air. A tear ran down his cheek.

"It's all gone. Everything's ruined."

That was when Helen realized the garden was in a shambles. It looked as though someone had tilled it up but in a haphazard fashion, the deep ruts going in every direction. Large paw prints in the dirt caught her attention.

"What happened?" she whispered.

"Coyotes. Maybe wolves," her daddy replied, though that didn't make sense. They were carnivores. Why would they tear into the dirt?

"I don't understand," Maggie said. "Don't they eat other animals?"

Their daddy glared at them. "Yes, but do you see the tracks? What else could it be?"

Both Helen and her siblings stared at their daddy in disbelief. He must have sensed their apprehension and snapped at them. "Get back in the house. All of you. I'll figure it out. Go!"

Helen jumped, then grabbing Maggie's hand, hurried back into the house.

Once inside, Helen's mother called out to them from the front parlor. "Maggie, is that you?"

"Yes, Momma. Helen too."

"Girls, can you bring me a cool washcloth? Hurry please."

Maggie looked at Helen, and both girls were confused at their mother's request. Once they brought it to their mother, they understood. It was Henry.

"Thank you, girls," their mother said. "He's burning up. I don't know what it is, but it hit him all of a sudden."

Henry's little body was pale. Sweat glistened on his forehead and soaked his shirt.

"Is there anything we can do, Mother?" Helen asked. A streak of worry creeped up her spine.

Her mother shook her head. "No dear, not at the moment. Wait. Aren't you supposed to be with your father?"

"The garden is ruined and daddy thinks a coyote did it. I think he's going to hunt for it," Maggie said.

"He told us to get inside," Helen added.

"I see. Why don't the two of you go play in your room while I try and bring Henry's fever down."

"Yes, ma'am," Helen said. She didn't wait for her mother to change her mind and grabbed Maggie's arm to direct her upstairs.

Four

"Are you sure about this?" Maggie asked.

Helen smiled. "Why not?"

"Because Mr. Argyle forbid us, and Daddy would be furious if he caught us."

"He won't be back for a while, and Mother is occupied with Henry."

Maggie wrung her hands. Between the two of them, Maggie was by far the rule follower; Helen was often the instigator. This time, she was goading her older sister into going up to the mysterious third floor, the one place of the house they were forbidden to go.

"But why?" Maggie asked. She had been stalling ever since Helen proposed they go up there after being dismissed by their daddy and then their mother.

"Because I'm bored and there's nothing else to do," Helen said.

Maggie sighed. The look in her eye was one Helen had seen before. It was the one that told her she was along for the adventure.

"Sure. But if we get caught, I'm blaming you."

Helen squealed and bolted up the creaky stairs.

Maggie hurried behind her.

Once they stepped into the hallway at the top of the stairs, Helen let out a whistle. Everything was coated in dust. It was like no one had touched the area in years, though it had only been a few weeks since Mr. Argyle left.

"It's so dirty," Maggie said. "Maybe Mr. Argyle wanted us to stay away because he hadn't had a chance to clean it before we arrived."

"Mother would never let this happen. She'd have us on our hands and knees scrubbing everything." A memory of her and Maggie cleaning the kitchen in their farmhouse back in Ulysses flashed in her mind. All she remembered was how sore her knees were from scrubbing on the floor all day.

"If she knew it was like this up here, she might make us clean it!" Maggie added.

"Then we better not tell her," Helen replied.

She took the lead, pulling on her sister's hand as she ventured into the darkened hallway.

Unlike the other two floors of the house, this one had very few windows. Sunlight struggled to penetrate much of the area, which gave it a more decrepit look than Helen thought possible. It was like an entirely different house, one she would never have wanted to live in had she known it was like this.

She tried the first door on their left, and it was locked. She rattled the handle a few times, but when Maggie clasped her shoulder to get her attention, her sister placed a finger to her lips and shushed her. "Mother will hear you."

Helen nodded her understanding and headed straight for the door across the hall.

This one opened.

Helen's eyes widened as she stared into the dark room. The window on the far side was completely covered with a sheet or blanket, and the dim light from the hallway didn't offer any help. Gulping her courage, she felt alongside the doorframe for a light switch. Her fingers found a small, round button and pushed.

A hum and buzz overhead was followed by a flickering light. It finally remained on, though it alternated from bright to dim before finally settling on dim.

The room was lined with bookcases filled with all kinds of books and odd objects. Helen gasped when she noticed a skull on one shelf, flanked on either side by red candles that had been used before, their sides coated in melted wax. Her skin prickled. Was it a real skull?

Maggie pushed past her to inspect the books, her fingers slowly touching the spines while she read their titles.

"None of these make sense. I can't understand the words," she said.

Helen approached, her eyes darting between her sister and the skull as though preparing for it to jump off the shelf after them.

All the words were in something other than English, and she wasn't sure what language they were.

"What is this place?" Helen asked.

"We probably shouldn't be in here," Maggie said. "I think we need to go."

Helen spotted something on the bottom shelf that caught her eye in the dim light of the room. She bent over and picked it up.

"What's that?" Maggie asked. It was the only thing in the room that had English letters on it. A board, sort of like a game board, had the alphabet printed on it in two rows. Underneath were the numbers one through zero. The words Yes and No were printed to either side of the word Ouija at the top of the board. A sun and moon were in the top two corners. At the bottom it read Goodbye, then the maker of the board underneath that—William Fuld, Baltimore, MD, USA.

Helen showed her sister the board.

"Ouija?" she asked. "I've heard of that. Isn't it some kind of tool to talk with the dead?"

Helen's eyes bulged. The dead? She glanced back down at the

board, and her heart quickened. Her arms shook. What did Maggie mean by talk with the dead?

"They aren't real," Maggie assured her. "They're a game. Do you think a device to talk to spirits would be sold to the public like that? It's all made up."

"How do you use it?" Helen asked.

"There should be a pointer that—" Maggie pushed past her and bent toward the shelf. When she rose, she held a cream-colored pointer with the word Ouija printed at the top. "This!" she said, holding it up to Helen's face. "We use this with the board, and it's supposed to help us talk to ghosts."

Helen's heart picked up its pace. She held in her hands the means to talk to ghosts?

"We should use it," Maggie said, her eyes brightening. "It's just a game, anyway."

"I don't know. Maybe coming up here wasn't the best idea. I thought we'd find interesting things, but not...not this," Helen said, indicating the board. It gave her the heebie-jeebies just touching it.

"Don't get a bee in your bonnet," Maggie said.

Helen looked down at the board, then to her sister. Maggie wouldn't intentionally hurt her. Besides, what harm could it really do? If the thing was the means to contact spirits, maybe they could ask them how to get the crops to grow or if there was hidden money in the place.

"Fine," Helen said. "But not in here." The hairs on the back of her neck stood on end and a chill filled the room. Something about it wasn't right.

"We'll bring it back down to our room," Maggie said. She clutched the pointer to her chest and headed out of the room. Helen followed the tracks on the dusty floor and trailed down the stairs after her sister.

"This is going to be a gasser," Maggie said when Helen entered the room. "Come on, close the door."

Her exuberance filled the space with a bright energy, calming Helen's fears about using a toy to speak with the spirits. Down here, away from the musty room upstairs, it seemed much more innocent, as though it truly were just a game. Her mood lightened a bit and the hesitation she felt moments ago slowly morphed into excitement, especially with Maggie's joyous smile.

Helen closed the door behind her and handed the board to Maggie, who sat on her bed with her legs crossed. She placed the board in front of her and set the plastic pointer in the center.

"Come on," she said, waving her hand at the bed. "Sit. Let's see if we can get this thing to work."

Helen sat across from her, the board between them.

"How do we use it?" Helen asked.

"We place our fingertips here," Maggie said, demonstrating on the pointer. "Then we ask questions. If I remember correctly about how to use it, the pointer moves on its own to different letters or to Yes or No."

"That's it?" Helen wasn't sure what she expected, but with a device that claimed it gave them the means to speak with the dead, she thought it had to do something more.

"That's it," Maggie replied. Her bright smile grew even larger, tamping down Helen's fears.

Helen gently placed her fingertips on the pointer and nodded to Maggie. "I'm ready."

FIVE

"IT'S NOT DOING ANYTHING," Helen said. Five minutes into their session with the Ouija board and the plastic piece sat there like a dead rat. She expected movement, words spelled out, anything.

Instead, she and Maggie were left staring at the board and the excitement slowly dissipating.

"Give it a minute," Maggie said.

Helen did. Then another one. Maybe there weren't any ghosts nearby or maybe...it was a stupid game after all, and they were suckers for thinking otherwise.

"Is there anyone out there?" Maggie asked. "If you are here, please let us know."

Helen sighed. It was the fifth time her sister asked the question with no response. Her bladder was tingling; she really needed to pee.

"Maggie, I need to—"

The pointer moved.

"Did you do that?" Helen asked, her eyes growing like large saucers.

"No," Maggie said, bouncing slightly on the bed. "It's moving!"

The girls watched as the pointer slid around in small circles on the board. Helen's fingertips were barely on it, and she marveled at the movement.

"Are you real?" Maggie asked. Helen thought it was a stupid question, but she couldn't think of anything better. The pointer shot across the board until it pointed to the word Yes. Helen let out a squeak.

"I swear, Maggie, if you're doing this..."

"I'm not, I promise!"

Helen stared into her eyes, trying to detect the lie, but Maggie's face didn't betray her. If she was lying, she was doing a great job of covering it up.

"What is your name?" Helen asked, trying to play along with her sister.

The pointer shifted and slowly spelled out the letters A-Z-R-I-E-L. Helen watched with her mouth agape while the pointer stopped at each letter.

"Azriel?" she said out loud. "Is your name Azriel?" The pointer drifted toward Yes.

"That's a weird name," Maggie grumbled.

Helen glared at her. If this thing was real, insulting it was not a great idea.

"Can you help us?" Helen asked. It was why they wanted to talk to the dead, anyway. The sooner they got an answer, the quicker she could stop using the board. Something felt wrong about connecting with the spirit of an unknown dead person.

The pointer moved slowly across the board until it spelled out a word, one agonizing letter at a time. R-E-C-K-O-N-I-N-G.

"Recko...reckoning?" Helen asked. "What's that?"

Maggie scrunched her face and squeezed her eyes shut in deep thought. Finally, she said, "I think it means someone has to pay. I heard it in Sunday school once. Like when someone did something bad, they had to pay for their sins."

The idea that this thing they were speaking with was telling them they had to do such a thing scared her. Helen let go of the pointer as though it was a venomous snake, though she feared it already bit her.

"Maggie, what does this mean?"

"I think it means we're done."

The two girls stared at the board. Helen felt her skin prickle. Had they actually spoken with a ghost or did they unknowingly move the pointer on their own, a sort of mass hypnosis kind of thing?

A dark, frightening presence settled on the room, like a heavy thundercloud that smothered everything. Helen shivered.

"Maggie?" she asked with a quivering voice. "Maggie, what's happening?"

"I don't know," she replied. Her voice carried the same sense of fear Helen felt.

"I think we did something wrong," Helen said.

Both girls jumped from the bed, knocking the Ouija board to the floor. The moment it struck the wood, the ominous presence dissipated, vanishing into nothingness and leaving behind an uncomfortable emptiness.

Helen's arms shook. Maggie stepped to her sister and wrapped her in a hug. Both girls clung to one another. Helen welcomed the comforting embrace, which helped calm her pounding heart.

"This was stupid," Maggie said. "Let's never do this again. Promise?"

Helen nodded her head, too afraid to speak.

"I'm sorry I made you use the board," Maggie said. "We won't try that again."

Six

Two days after using the Ouija board, Helen was awakened by the howls of a banshee. She bolted upright in her bed. Maggie did the same.

"What is that?" Helen asked. Both girls listened intently as the wailing grew more pronounced. Whatever it was, pain carried in the sound. Helen's first thought was maybe it was the spirit from the board, which had been silent ever since they used it. Maybe it was in their house, spreading evil.

"I think..." Maggie said, rubbing the sleep from her eyes, "I think it's Momma. Come on." Maggie got out of bed and reached for her sister's hand. Helen held it back at first, but with Maggie's insistence, she relented, and the two girls left their room.

They followed the source of the horrific crying downstairs, where they found their parents bent over their little brother Henry.

"What's wrong?" Helen asked. She startled her parents. It was her daddy who spoke.

"Your brother," he said in a shaky voice, "he's dead."

Grief pierced Helen's heart so quickly and thoroughly that she collapsed to her knees and sobbed. Maggie did the same, the two girls clutching each other for comfort.

"No," Helen whispered.

"Daddy," Maggie said, "what happened to Henry?"

Their mother looked up with a dirty faced streaked with tears. "The sickness caught up to him. He just…stopped breathing."

Helen's thoughts turned immediately to the weird word the spirit shared with them on the Ouija board: reckoning. Could this have anything to do with that? Could she and her sister somehow have been responsible for their brother's death? Just the possibility of it brought on such a crushing sense of guilt that she went speechless.

Her other brothers, Robert and Charlie, stumbled out of their bedroom, rubbing sleep from their eyes.

"Momma?" Robert asked. He glanced at Helen and Maggie, then back to his mother. "What's wrong?"

"Henry," Helen said, trying to muster the courage to speak. It took her a moment before she could continue. "He's dead."

"What? No!" He and Charlie both raced to their mother. Their daddy stood between them.

"It ain't no use, sons. He's gone." Their daddy had always refused to cry, and even with their dead brother in their mother's arms, his face was a statue. Tight lips. Distant gaze. To Helen, it was as though he didn't register the truth of what happened to Henry.

"We need to bury him," he said, as though it were the most natural thing to say about your own son.

"Boys, grab shovels in the barn and come around near the pond out back." When the pair refused to move, he scolded them. "I said now! You need to move before I whip the both of you."

They glanced at their mother, and when she nodded, they ran off to do as they were told.

Helen and Maggie held each other as their mother sobbed with Henry's lifeless body in her arms. Helen felt sick, like a massive hole had opened in her heart. She had no proof but felt certain what she and Maggie did with the spirit had something to do with their brother's death, no matter what their mother said.

Close to an hour later, Helen stood staring at a freshly-dug mound of dirt that enveloped her brother's body. Standing next to her were her siblings and her parents, all of them with tears running down their faces.

"We never should've left Kansas," their mother said. "Henry never would've gotten sick."

"You don't know that, Bea. He could have caught something else. The boy's constitution wasn't strong enough," their father replied.

The six of them stood in silence for a long time, Helen using the moments to reflect on her brother and what she possibly did to have made his death happen. It was an unsettling feeling, and she knew she had to do something to fix it.

SEVEN

LATER THAT DAY, Helen pulled the Ouija board out from under her bed and set it on her lap. Maggie had her back turned to her and was sleeping after having spent all her energy grieving for her dead brother. Helen tapped the box. Calling out to the dead spirit might bring answers about her brother. Maybe...maybe they could speak with Henry himself. She could apologize for what she did. The prospect of reaching him grew more powerful in her mind. She placed the box on the bed next to her and approached Maggie, intending on waking her up.

"Maggie?" she said in a quiet voice as she gently shook her. "Maggie, we need to try something."

Her sister groaned and rolled to face her. "What do you want?" she muttered.

"Henry. We can try to talk to Henry."

"He's dead," Maggie said.

"The board. We can try it."

Maggie's eyes narrowed and her lips pursed together. "Don't you think that was the reason he died to begin with? We messed with a force we don't understand," Maggie said.

"We have to try."

Maggie pushed herself up until she was seated and let out a deep sigh. "Sure, we can try."

The two girls placed their hands on the pointer. Helen closed her eyes for a moment to focus on her younger brother, trying to get a clear picture of his face in her mind. Concentrating on him, she asked out loud, "Henry, are you here? Henry, it's Helen and Maggie. We want to talk to you. We want to say we're sorry."

She and Maggie peered at the pointer, waiting for it to move.

"Henry, please, if you are here, talk to us. We didn't mean for anything bad to happen," Helen said.

"We had no idea," Maggie added.

Slowly, the pointer started to move. Helen's heart raced in her chest. "Henry, is that you?" she asked.

The pointer moved slowly toward No.

She looked to Maggie, and both of them seemed confused.

"Are you...Azriel?" Maggie asked. The pointer slid across the board until it rested on Yes.

"What did you do to our brother? He was innocent! He was just a little child!" Helen scolded. She didn't mean to yell at the spirit, but her emotions took hold of her.

The pointer suddenly flew from their hands and shot across the room until it smacked into the door and fell to the floor. Both girls let out a shriek.

Loud footsteps hurried to their room. Helen shoved the box and board under her bed just as the door flung open. It was their daddy.

"What's going on in here?" he asked. His eyes were red, and Helen swore she noticed streaks through the dirt on his face. The pointer lay on the floor at his feet. He noticed it, picking it up and carefully inspecting it. "What is this? Where did it come from?" He glared at the both of them. "Answer me!"

"I found it, Daddy," Helen said.

"Where did you get it? Was there anything else with it?"

She guessed he meant the board. "No, sir," she lied. "Just...just that thing."

"Maggie?" he asked, pointing it at her.

She hesitated, and Helen figured she was found out.

"She's telling the truth, Daddy. It was in the closet."

He eyed both of them. Helen knew he was skeptical of their story, but he didn't push it.

"Don't go messing with this thing, do you hear me?"

"Yes, Daddy," they said in unison.

He took the pointer and shoved it in his back pocket. "You girls need to help your mother with things around the house for a little while. She's gonna need both of you." He turned and closed the door as he left.

Helen covered her face with her hands and cried.

"That board is evil," Maggie said. "We never should have played with it."

Helen wiped the tears from her eyes. "I didn't know."

Maggie crossed the room and wrapped Helen in her arms. The two girls sat like that for a long time. Helen couldn't get her mind off of her dead brother and what role she might have played in his death. It made her sick thinking what she and Maggie had done with the Ouija board actually caused such a horrific accident.

Eight

THAT NIGHT, Helen was awakened by heavy footsteps on the hardwood floors outside her room. They sounded clumsy, like when her daddy came back from visiting a speakeasy. Yet they were also not as thunderous as her daddy.

A groan sounded in the hall outside her door and she shivered.

"Maggie. Maggie, are you awake?" she whispered, fearing if she was any louder, whoever was outside their door might hear her.

"Yes," she replied.

"What is that?" Helen asked.

"I don't know."

A loud knock on their door forced Helen to squeal, and she covered her mouth to silence herself. The knock continued.

Finally, someone spoke. "Maggie? Hewen?" The voice was soft and like a little child.

The way her name was mispronounced could only mean one person. "Henry?" Helen asked. "Henry, is that you?"

"Hewen? I so cold."

Throwing off the blanket, she raced to the door and flung it open.

Henry stood facing her, his entire body caked in dirt. A worm wriggled out of his ear and plopped to the floor.

Helen gasped.

Maggie stood just behind her.

"Henry, are you ok?" Helen asked. She was afraid to get too close to him. It was her little brother, but something was off about him. Something wasn't quite right.

"Hewen?" he asked in his simple way. "I'm cold."

Helen was too stunned to move. How could her brother be standing in the hallway? She was there when they buried him. How could he be alive? It was impossible.

"Blankie," Henry said. Dirt flew from his lips when he spoke. His eyes were dark, blacker than anything she had ever seen. This was her brother, but clearly *not* her brother.

Maggie pulled Helen back into the room, and Henry stepped forward, crossing the threshold and leaving muddy footprints on the floor.

"Cold," Henry said. "So cold."

A grin creased his dirt-caked face, and it twisted into a snarl. Henry lunged at the sisters, who let out a blood-curdling scream.

Helen escaped her little brother's attack, but Maggie did not. Despite being dead, Henry attacked with a ferociousness that shocked Helen. She couldn't move while Henry mauled their sister.

The little boy growled and snarled, digging his dirty fingers into Maggie's mouth and pulling at her soft cheeks. She cried out, but Henry didn't seem to care. Instead, he bit her cheek and yanked his head back, tearing her soft flesh. Blood sprayed from the wound, Maggie's cries exacerbating the injury.

"Henry, no!" Helen yelled, coming back to her senses. She grabbed his shoulders to yank him off, but he resisted her attempts with a strength he never should have possessed. He pushed her back, and she stumbled until she smashed into the wall.

Henry turned his attention back to Maggie and attacked her.

Blood sprayed into the air. Henry continued to growl like a

rabid dog, biting and tearing pieces of her flesh. Maggie screamed louder and louder.

Their bedroom door flung open, smacking into Helen. It was their daddy! He had a large stick in one hand. Their mom and her other brothers were right behind him.

"What's going on?" their daddy asked. His eyes bulged, then he let out a primal yell at the sight of their youngest sibling attacking their oldest.

He rushed across the room, dropping the stick, and ripped Henry free. The boy's face was covered in blood and gore. Maggie convulsed on the floor. Their mother pushed past their daddy and Henry to attend to Maggie. Helen watched all of this with her mouth agape and words failing to form on her tongue. With the massive, bleeding wound on Maggie's neck, she knew there was no way her sister would survive this.

Her daddy yelled, and Henry dropped from his grip. The boy scurried around like a wild animal, avoiding her daddy's attempt to capture him. Henry snarled and lunged; the force of his little body with its unnatural strength slamming into her daddy's knee was devastating. His knee snapped, a sickening crunch sounded, and he collapsed to the floor. Henry turned to their two other brothers and lunged at them. He caught Robert's neck and squeezed, while his other hand found Charlie's eyes. He plunged his dirty fingers into Charlie's eyes and soon forced them to burst. Charlie screamed. Henry continued to hold Robert in a terrible chokehold, and no matter how hard Robert beat on Henry's arm, her little brother never let go.

Their mother screamed at Henry. "Stop it! Leave your brothers alone!"

Henry snarled and squeezed harder. Robert fought a little longer, but his face turned a dark shade and soon his efforts stopped. Henry tossed him aside easily.

Charlie screamed and wailed, blood and ichor leaking down his face. Where his eyes used to be were bloody pockets.

"Henry, stop!" Helen screamed.

Ignoring her, her little brother jammed his fingers farther back into Charlie's skull. Grabbing his head like a ball, Henry shoved it backward until Charlie flew across the hall and slammed into the far wall. He fell to the floor in a heap, blood oozing from his broken face.

Their mother ran after Henry. "Stop this!" she screamed. Henry turned toward her, and she backhanded him, sending him across the room from the vicious blow. But it did not stop their little brother.

He scrambled back to his feet and crawled on all fours like an evil crab until he reached their mother. She stood with wide eyes and a pale face, her mouth open and her arms trembling.

"Henry, please. You must stop this. We are your family."

An evil grin crossed their little brother's face, and he leaped at their mother, knocking her down. She screamed, but he was undaunted by her cries. Henry mauled her, tearing large chunks of hair from her skull and slinging them to the side. One piece was so full of flesh and blood that it stuck to the wall.

Their mother howled.

Helen broke from her stupor to rush at her little brother. He flung out his thin arm and brushed her aside. The strength in his movement surprised Helen. There was no way he should've been capable of that. She fell to the floor, and Henry turned back to their mother. Her screams filled the room as Henry tore into her. Blood and gore sprayed up into the air, the sickly smell of fresh death permeating everything.

Helen pushed herself away from Henry. Her daddy managed to get to his feet, his one leg bent at a horrifying angle, the part below his knee sticking out like a wild hair after sleeping all night.

"Henry!" he shouted. "Leave! This is not your home anymore."

Henry ignored him, attacking their mother and opening a massive wound on her abdomen. Helen swore she saw her insides, and it made her sick.

Their daddy hobbled toward Henry using the stick he had earlier as a cane, the boy not paying any bit of attention. When he got close enough, Helen noticed tears running down her daddy's face, leaving streaks in the blood.

"I'm so sorry," he muttered. With a shout, her daddy swung the stick like a baseball bat. The horrific sound as wood connected with bone made Helen scream. Henry fell to the side and their daddy struck him again.

Henry convulsed on the floor. His limbs vibrated. They thumped repeatedly on the wooden beams. Their daddy struck again, large tears falling from his eyes as he swung the stick over and over.

The heavy thud as the wood connected with her brother made Helen cry out. She covered her eyes but couldn't stop the sound of the attack.

Moments later, the beating stopped. The only sound that remained was that of her daddy breathing heavily. She opened her eyes and gasped.

Her mother was clearly dead. The large, gaping wound in her belly left no room for doubt.

Henry was dead. Again. Her daddy beat him so badly that his head was flat.

By the looks of it, she assumed Maggie, Robert, and Charlie were also dead.

All that was left was her and her daddy.

A powerful sense of guilt enveloped her. Helen couldn't hold back the tears. She caused this! She knew it had something to do with that stupid Ouija board she and Maggie played with. Azriel. Didn't the spirit say its name was Azriel? Somehow, she and Maggie must've unleashed the evil being and it brought her little brother back from the dead and now all of her family was dead. All but her daddy. That was the only explanation for the evil she just witnessed. It sounded crazy, but it had to be true.

NINE

HELEN and her daddy left soon after the incident. It was a struggle, but her daddy was able to drive them to the local hospital to get his leg fixed and have Helen checked out. He sent a telegram to Mr. Argyle that they were leaving and he would find a way to pay him back for the advance they were given. What her daddy didn't do was alert the authorities about their family. He told Helen no one would believe them.

Two weeks after the horrific events, Helen and her daddy came back to the house to collect their belongings and bury the dead.

"Daddy, I'm scared," Helen said as they pulled into the driveway.

He turned to look at her in the back seat. "Be brave. We have to do this so their spirits have peace."

She slowly nodded, knowing he was right, but it didn't make it any better.

They exited the car and were up the steps to the house when the front door creaked open. Helen's heart thundered in her chest with the worry that somehow her little brother had come back to life...again.

Instead, it was Mr. Argyle who stepped onto the porch.

Her daddy gasped. "Mr. Argyle, I...we..."

The strange man held up a hand. "I know what you did. I warned you not to go into my quarters." He peered at Helen. "Does the name Azriel mean anything to you?"

She felt the blood run from her cheeks. A chill ran up her spine and made the hairs on the back of her neck stand on end.

"I thought so," Mr. Argyle said. "Once summoned, Azriel requires a host. It is never wise to play with things that you do not understand."

Helen's daddy looked down at her, a confused look on his face. "What does he mean?" he asked.

"The girl let curiosity get hold of her, and for that, others have died. Keep the money, Mr. Cartwright. I have taken care inside the house; you do not need to worry. What happened here at Argyle Manor will never be spoken of again. Take your daughter and go. The Model T is yours as well. Speak no more about what you experienced here. Stay silent and all will be well. If you share this with anyone," he said, peering at Helen and making her shrink back from the man, "then you will suffer a fate worse than death."

"But Mr. Argyle," her daddy protested, "my family—"

Mr. Argyle held up a hand to silence him. "I have everything under control. I'm afraid their bodies cannot be moved from the property. I suggest you go far from here and never return. Azriel is not a kind spirit."

For several long moments, they stood facing one another. Finally, her daddy took a step back. "I understand," he muttered.

"Live well and keep quiet. Love each other as you loved all your family." Mr. Argyle turned and headed inside, closing the door behind him.

Sniffling and wiping his eyes, her daddy placed a hand on Helen's back. "Come, let's do as he said."

Helen wiped at her own tears. "I'm sorry, Daddy. I didn't know."

He didn't say a word as they walked back to the car and climbed inside. When her daddy turned on the engine, Helen clung to the door, her face pressed against the glass. Her daddy shifted into drive and turned around in the driveway.

The entire time, Mr. Argyle stared at Helen from inside the house. She didn't know if she should wave or hurl insults at the man. Thinking better of it, she did nothing as her daddy drove away from Argyle Manor.

They had come there to escape the poverty and the horrible dust in Kansas. They were leaving with most of her family dead and a large wound inside of her because of her guilt. It felt like the worst trade in history, and she had no one to blame but herself.

ACHIEVEMENT
UNLOCKED

KILLBOI97X LEANED BACK IN HIS CURVED, BLACK GAMING CHAIR. Energy drinks littered the floor next to him. After sitting so long, his back ached.

"Stupid game. Lag screwed me." He ended second in the match, with a score of 15-2. "I shoulda been first."

"Whatever, man, you crushed it," his friend SlimBat52 said over the headset.

Killboi97x played seven straight days of nothing but online death-matches, grinding toward the last achievement he needed. He invested over eighty hours in the game since he got it two weeks ago. At that rate, it would be another two weeks to grind out enough kills for the achievement.

"Yeah, whatever, I'm bored with this, anyway. I'll get the achievement, but it's gonna suck," Killboi97x said.

SlimBat52 snickered over the headset.

"You know what would be awesome? If this was real. I'd love to put a bullet in the idiot that stole my last kill. Screw him," Killboi97x said.

"Dude, shut the hell up with that bullshit."

"No way. I'd headshot that idiot."

Static and silence followed.

"Adam, are you for real?" SlimBat52 said, using Killboi's real name. Adam and Lee—SlimBat52—had been friends since junior high. Adam owned opponents in every shooter game they played, but he never proposed something like this. "Have you ever shot a real gun?" Lee asked.

"Why not? We've got the practice."

"Yeah, but not with real people or real guns."

"Come on, Lee. Think about it. Targets are everywhere. Couldn't we find a few to lose? Maybe the homeless? There's always a bunch at the corner near my apartment. We could make our own game, with an achievement for how many kills we get or how we kill them."

Lee hesitated. "How about that last achievement?" he said, trying to turn the conversation. "I can help for another hour or so, then I gotta get some sleep."

"Yeah, sure," Adam said, dropping the subject. He clicked over to his achievement list, the final trophy icon shaded darker than the rest. He would get it. He had to. Leaving it locked wasn't an option.

"Man, I'm tired. I'm gonna go. We can play again tomorrow," Lee said after two-and-a-half more hours of playing.

"Cool. I'm gonna keep working at this achievement. Gonna try to get halfway there before I jump off. Lee—" he said, pausing, "remember what we talked about. I think we can do it."

A click indicated Lee left the chat.

Three hours later, Adam turned off his console. He rubbed his strained eyes with sore hands. He wasn't quite halfway like he hoped, but he was closer. An organized clan annihilated his team of random players who were more concerned with shooting each other than the enemy. The last few matches were tedious. *I can't wait till I hit that achievement. I hate this game. It's the same thing over and over again. There's no thrill anymore.*

Adam decided it was time to capture the thrill again.

The next day, he surprised Lee by showing up at his house. Lee opened the door, and by way of introduction, Adam moved his coat to reveal a six-cylinder Colt Python.

"Whoa, what the hell, man," Lee said. His eyes widened. He stepped back.

Adam laughed.

"I told you, games bore me. Let's do it for real. Five headshots, no ammo refill—achievement unlocked."

"No way, Adam, that's crazy. That's murder! Where'd you get the gun, anyway?"

"It's not crazy. It's a game."

"People don't come back. They don't respawn. You shoot, you kill. And then prison. This is wrong."

Adam drew the pistol from his waistband, holding it casually, turning it side to side as if inspecting a new toy.

"What are you doing? Put that away! What if my neighbors see it?" Lee said, shifting from one foot to the other, his eyes never leaving the pistol in Adam's hand.

With a fluid motion, Adam grasped the pistol, pointed, and fired.

Brain and bone splattered on the wall behind Lee. A bloody, gaping hole was left in his forehead. His body fell to the floor. Adam dropped the gun from the kickback and clutched his ears.

"Ow! That's so freaking loud!" He looked down at his friend, a dark, thick crimson halo radiating beneath his head.

"Lee? Lee, get up. Come on, Lee, get up. It's a game. It's just a game."

When Lee didn't move, Adam retrieved the pistol, shoved it in his pants, and ran. He hid under a bridge downtown. He envisioned one glowing neon-green tick mark. Four shaded tick marks called to him, mocked him, teased him. "Four more, that's all I need. When Lee respawns, maybe he'll play the game."

Adam didn't return home, afraid he would get spawn killed by the enemy. In order to win, he would need to stay aggressive and be wary of dangers. Potential targets and enemies scouting for him lurked everywhere.

He ran behind buildings or hid behind cars when he felt threatened. Never before had he been so connected to a game. He had an achievement to unlock, and he was gonna see it through.

His second and third kills were a couple strolling through the park. He camped, waiting for them to approach. Hidden within a bush, he shot the man and then the woman, both in the head. The adrenaline was electric, like playing the newest game for the first time before anyone else. Excitement built as he progressed toward the achievement. Three tick marks of the five glowed green.

His next kill was an old man hobbling with a cane in an alley. The confused look on the man's face when Adam raised the pistol was wiped away with one bullet. Adam grinned, watching the old man lay on the street. One more. He was one more kill away from obtaining the achievement.

He roamed the streets searching for his final kill. With two bullets left in his gun and no ammo refill, he had to pick the perfect target.

"I'm Killboi!" he yelled at a woman walking her dog as sunset neared, waving his gun in the air. He considered her for his last kill.

She screamed and ran the other direction, pulling her barking dog with her.

"Hey, don't move! Drop the weapon!" an officer called. He must have been on patrol, just out of sight.

Adam ran. He knocked into a few onlookers as he flew past. He wanted to stop running; he wasn't in the best shape. But the achievement wasn't unlocked. He had one more to go.

Adam spun around the corner and stopped cold. Dead end. Dull yellow light flickered over a row of dumpsters lining the short street. He hid behind the last one and waited in the cover of the growing darkness.

Footsteps echoed in the alley and stopped. "This is 99871 requesting backup at the intersection of 130th and Lena. Armed suspect in the vicinity," the officer said. The radio crackled in response.

Adam shifted his foot, and a bottle rolled into the street.

"Engaging suspect," the officer said.

Quick footsteps grew closer to Adam. When the officer turned toward him with his weapon drawn, Adam pointed the Python at him. His trained finger squeezed the trigger, firing one shot in the officer's head.

"Yes!" he yelled as the body dropped. "I did it!" He sat against the building, staring at his victory in front of him.

In the distance, sirens warned of more trouble, but he did it. *I unlocked the achievement!*

The fleeting satisfaction of winning slipped away. There was nothing left to try. He unlocked the almost-unobtainable achievement. What could possibly top it?

Cars screeched at the alley's entrance. Sirens blared. The sound of footsteps grew closer.

Adam held the gun to his head.

A dozen officers filed into the alley, guns drawn.

"Freeze! Put down your weapon!" an officer demanded.

Adam looked at the body, then to the officers facing him.

One bullet remained in his gun. He craved the victorious high he felt moments earlier. He would have to restart the game and try again.

"Achievement unlocked," he said.

Adam pulled the trigger, ending the game.

THE FOREVER CABIN

I SANK INTO A SOFT FAKE-LEATHER COUCH TRIMMED IN A ROUGH fabric. It enveloped me, though honestly, I hated those kinds of cushions. But it was the perfect place to enjoy the cabin. The chocolate-brown couch contrasted with the light oak walls and ceiling. Olive-green painted trim around the windows and doors completed the rustic ambiance.

Enjoying my morning coffee, I heard the wind blow through the pines outside. Random creaking throughout the cabin hinted at something moving, maybe the wind pushing against small boards or catching on the roof.

The otherwise silence within the cabin left me too much time with my thoughts about the last twelve months.

IT STARTED when my wife left me last year, taking our two kids and three cats with her. She claimed I spent far too much time worried more about work than the family, though as an emergency physician, what the hell else was I supposed to do? She wanted a certain lifestyle, and my job afforded those luxuries. Make no mistake, I loved my work. Giving back to people and helping them heal gave me a rush. But after the divorce, I couldn't concentrate, and after one horribly-botched bone setting (ever seen an arm twist back on itself?), I quit to recover my senses. I had money stashed away and would be fine for about a year, even with child support.

I found the cabin on Airbnb and immediately fell in love with it. I had never used a service like it, but the process was smooth. I packed up my Corvette and headed west, leaving Missouri for Arizona. I took two days to drive out, stopping at places and attractions my wife, Beth, would've never stopped at. I gained a sense of freedom with each stop, something I hadn't had in a long time.

I arrived at the cabin on a Thursday. I whistled when I opened the door to my retreat. Large enough to comfortably house eight people, it also included an attached two-car garage. It was overkill for just one guest. The view from the wraparound porch was what really attracted me when I spotted it online. The rest I could care less about.

I made my rounds of the place, checking out every room and marveling at the large oak poles used for ceiling joists and columns throughout. The walls were made of similar logs. All of it was a light pine color, probably from the surrounding Ponderosa pine forests of Northern Arizona. I enjoyed how the cabin felt like it was out in the wilderness despite being five minutes from the nearby town of Williams.

Depositing my suitcase in the master bedroom downstairs, I hopped into the shower to wash off the grime of the road and settled in for the night.

I slept horribly that first night. I hadn't grown accustomed to the random creaks and groans of the cabin. Each breeze woke me, and I feared an intruder. Call it my city upbringing with a constant fear of crime. Either way, by the time the sun came up and the birds called out, my tired body protested when I decided to get up and start the day.

I went to the kitchen to brew coffee and figure out what to have for breakfast.

Damn, I thought. I got in kinda late the night before and hadn't stopped for supplies. The only thing in the cupboard was a small can of decaf coffee, a useless product if there ever was one. I rubbed my eyes, and a voice cursed me in my head.

That's just stupid, Luke. Why would you not go to the store? It's because you were too busy stopping every few minutes to take a piss or chase after young girls. The voice was Beth's, and her words cut deeply. The tone was familiar, and that made it worse. Near the end of our marriage, she accused me of infidelity in that same voice. As it turned out, she was the one cheating on me. And with a fucking janitor!

I cursed at her in the silent cabin.

Throwing on my clothes, I went into Williams and ate breakfast at a local place on Route 66 known for having some of the best food in town. I couldn't help but enjoy the meal and forget Beth's scathing voice from earlier.

After breakfast, I found a grocery store and stocked up on all the necessities, most importantly coffee, water, and whiskey. And some food. I didn't find joy in cooking, but I intended on staying at the cabin as much as possible over my five-day stay, so the more food I had, the less I needed to travel into town.

Beth used to get on to me about what I ate. She would've hated the things I brought back. But who was I trying to impress? I hadn't been with another woman since her, and alone in the cabin, I hadn't anticipated that changing.

After putting everything away, I took a nap because I could do whatever the hell I wanted to do. When I woke up, I grabbed a notebook and pen and headed out the back door to the covered deck and the warm sunshine.

For years I thought I should write a book. I was a big fan of King and Ramsey Campbell, and in a moment of self-delusion, I bought a leatherbound notebook and a nice pen that wrote in blue ink from a tourist-trap gas station in New Mexico, thinking having these tools was my first step to becoming a famous writer. Beth used to laugh at me when I shared my desire to one day write a book. She thought I should stick with my day job and quit wasting time daydreaming about something I would never do because I had a history of not finishing what I started. I guess this was going to be my attempt at proving her wrong.

I sat out on the deck and listened to the breeze filter through the pines surrounding the cabin. At that time of day, the birds had finally quieted, and the only other sound was that of squirrels running up and down the trees.

In the shade of the covered deck, the heat clung to me like I was under a large magnifying glass hidden from view. It was a dry heat though, which helped keep the sweat away. Humidity sucked back home in St. Louis. This higher elevation with crazy-low humidity helped clear my head, because I had a lot going on in there.

I sat the notebook on my lap and closed my eyes, inhaling the deep scent of pine. I thought of Beth and the life I once lived.

Something changed our relationship well before the infidelity, and I never could get a good grasp of what that was. I used to adore her, worshipping her every movement. Her laugh made my heart sing. Her smile warmed even the coldest of days. But then it all changed.

Beth scowled more than she smiled. Her eyes no longer carried light and life, but rather darkness and betrayal. Looking back, I saw that. At the time, I had no idea what it was. She claimed it was her fibromyalgia. I believed her. She had been dealing with it for over ten years. Turns out she was using her situation to manipulate me so she could screw around with a guy behind my back. When I confronted her about it, she came clean.

"You've been so distant," she said. "I wanted nothing more than to be with you, but every time I tried, you fell further away."

I tried talking my way out of the impending breakup, but my anger took over. Imagining my wife screwing another man, spreading her legs for him and asking him to fuck her harder made me sick. I couldn't stand the thought of it.

So why did it still bother me? *Because you love her*, I answered myself. It was true. I did. Or at least I thought I did. But what did I know? Maybe I was wrong about my feelings.

A loud crash in the trees shattered my thoughts, and my eyes popped open. Jumping from my chair, the notebook tumbled to the deck.

"What's that?" I asked out loud, as though anyone was near to answer. The sound of the wind rustled through the needles of the surrounding pines. A bird screeched in the distance. I placed a hand over my heart, feeling it thud against my chest.

You're hearing things, I said to myself. I shook my head and collected my notebook. When my heart settled down, I stepped inside for a quick drink. Maybe my nerves were more on edge than I allowed myself to believe.

After two shots of smooth Irish whiskey, I felt better. The warmth inside nearly matched the temperature outside. I went back to the deck and opened the notebook, pen in hand, ready to knock out the words I had wanted to share for so long.

But they never came. It was like a dark curtain draped over my mind and stifled any coherent thought. I tried forcing the words, but I got maybe three sentences written. They were garbled and messy. None of it made sense.

"Fuck!" I screamed to the wilderness, half expecting the sudden outburst to clear my head and give me the impetus to start.

Moments later, the inspiration failed to arrive. Maybe it was the sudden noise earlier that startled me? I hadn't been able to concentrate since then. Or maybe it was the whiskey?

Knowing my time would be better spent doing anything else, I closed the notebook and set it on the small table next to me. I leaned back and closed my eyes, listening to the wind and enjoying the calm breeze.

I must've fallen asleep, because when I opened my eyes, everything was dark. The birds no longer chirped, replaced instead by the distant sounds of owls and coyotes.

What the hell? I thought. But then I smiled. What did it matter? My whole reason for being at this cabin in the first place was to relax and recalibrate my head. I could do whatever I wanted.

I opened the door to go back inside when a shrill cry split the darkness, settling at the base of my spine. My blood ran cold. My legs involuntarily shook. I wanted to turn toward the source, but my head refused to comply with my request. Forcing the issue, I turned slowly. I could see nothing in the inky forest. Though the moon shined bright, its reflection dared not enter the boughs of the trees.

Again the hellish sound called out, like an angel with its wings slowly and deliberately ripped from its body.

I ran into the cabin and slammed the door shut behind me. With my chest heaving, I leaned against the door. Even through the thick wood, the piercing cry curdled my blood. I hurriedly locked the door…and waited.

The cries continued for another fifteen minutes. I wished more than once I had a gun with me. As much as I detested what they did to my patients, at that moment, it was the only thing that would keep me safe from the mysterious creature outside.

Just as suddenly as it started, the horrible sound ended, leaving an echo in my ears.

I waited in the gloomy cabin for it to start up again. When a half hour passed and the deafening silence overcame me, I rushed to the cabinet and pulled off the lid to the whiskey. Tipping the bottle up, I let the amber liquid scald my throat.

It didn't take long for the alcohol to take effect. I needed my senses dulled in the worst way. With my mind retreating to my failed marriage and the wild sounds, I wanted to be anywhere else. The whiskey helped.

Not long after draining the bottle, I passed out again. This time, I did so on the large, overstuffed couch in front of the stone fireplace.

I awoke a few hours later with an immense urge to piss. I stumbled to the bathroom, going down the short hallway under the loft. When I plopped back down on the couch, I looked up into the dark loft.

My eyes widened. My breath quickened. Standing on the landing above and leaning against the wooden rail was a gorgeous woman. She had long brown hair with just the slightest wave to it. She wore a flowing black dress that seemed to glow around the edges. And her smile...it melted my jaded heart. She looked down at me and offered a slight wave. I guessed she was maybe in her late twenties. Her alabaster skin contrasted with her dress, and the low-cut front showed just enough cleavage to be revealing without showing too much.

"Who are you?" I mumbled, though I couldn't in all honesty say it was coherent. I felt my head swim, and the room had a slight spin to it. I closed my eyes for a brief moment, and when my gaze returned to the loft, the woman was gone. I rubbed my eyes, and the struggle to remain conscious failed badly.

I awoke to warm rays of sunshine beating down on my face. My head ached fiercely. Slowly, I sat up, and the mistake of the motion became evident as my stomach lurched and I vomited on myself. The digested remains of my stomach splashed all over me and the wooden floors. I wiped the strands of vomit-infused saliva from my chin and looked upward at the loft. Though I didn't remember much about getting drunk, I did remember her, the ghostly woman of the loft.

The woman's appearance startled me, yet at the same time, I was entirely transfixed by her. I had never seen someone so beautiful and majestic in my life. I would love to say my ex-wife was such a person, but maybe my attitude soured after what she did to me.

I still wasn't sure who the woman was or why she appeared to me. *It's all in your head*, I thought.

My stomach lurched. My body threatened to expunge its contents again, and in my struggle to maintain myself, I forgot all about the woman.

Several hours later, after a hot shower and copious amounts of starchy food, I could think straight again.

I grabbed a glass of water and sat back on the cleaned couch, the faint aroma of vomit wafting up from the cushions. I had my notebook with me as well, hoping to gain inspiration to write though my attention was drawn back to the loft. I wanted the woman to appear. I desperately wished she would show once more.

The evening passed in relative silence, and my body ached too much for me to do anything. Giving up the chance to see her, I slowly plodded to the downstairs bedroom to sleep off the remains of my powerful hangover.

Sometime in the middle of the night, I heard a creaking sound. I thought someone was walking on the main floor. Instantly my heart thudded inside my chest. Then the screams I heard the night before once again erupted outside the cabin. I felt surrounded, like I had no escape from whatever it was that wanted me.

I pulled the comforter up to my chin as though it could save me from the terrors beyond, whether they were real or not.

The creaking noise grew louder and more deliberate, very much like a person walking toward me.

"Who's out there?" I shouted, doing my best to sound confident and strong. The creaking stopped. "I swear I'll shoot!" I lied.

A scream carried through the walls, which nearly made me jump from the bed. They grew more intense and soon surrounded the cabin on all sides. The loud disturbance disoriented me, making me lose focus on the creaking, which I soon realized started up again.

"Stop it. I swear I have a gun!"

I jumped from the bed, pulling on the sweatpants I left on the dresser. Fumbling in the darkness, I almost tripped when I put my leg in. At the last second, I caught myself with a hand against the wooden log wall.

The creaking grew heavier and louder as though from right outside my closed door. "Don't come in here or I'll shoot," I lied.

I scanned the dark room, looking for anything to use as a weapon. I panicked when the doorknob turned, the brass glinting in the moonlight.

The cries outside stopped. The door swung open softly.

"Luke?" a delicate female voice called out. "Luke, are you ok?"

A confused thought raced through my head. "Beth?" I mumbled, unsure of myself.

"Luke, what's going on?" The overhead light blazed to life, and I shielded my eyes. When they adjusted, I rubbed them several times to make sure I was seeing what I thought I saw.

"Beth? What are you doing here?"

Standing in the doorway was my ex-wife, in the flesh. She was dressed in a pair of black shorts and a light-pink tank top. She wore her long hair in a tight ponytail.

"Luke, we've been so worried."

"We?" I had no idea what she meant. Was it really her? Was I in a dream within a dream?

"Me and the girls. I heard about your job. I'm so sorry."

I honestly had no response. I both loved and hated Beth. I wanted to kiss and strangle her, the chasm between the two reactions growing smaller every minute.

"Daddy!" my two girls said. They ran to me, wrapping their arms around me. In a few years, when they would become teenagers, they would never want a damn thing to do with me.

"Audry and Caroline were worried sick. I told them everything was all right, but…is it? Are you ok?"

Her mock concern ignited my anger.

"Why the fuck would you care?"

"Luke, not in front of the girls."

I glared at my daughters. The look of fear and repulsion they gave me cut deeply into my soul. They backed away as though fearing my touch would turn them into something horrid and repugnant. I wiped my face, and when I removed my hands, they were gone.

My mind raced with the meaning of the encounter.

"Beth? Girls? Where…where are you?"

In response, the shrill cry from outside the cabin answered me. The hairs on the back of my neck stood on end. Goosebumps covered my arms.

"Stop it!"

The cabin creaked. I swore it sounded close to falling in on itself.

As suddenly as all the madness started, it ended. A silent void filled the cabin. Nothing stirred.

I stumbled from the room and entered the kitchen. I needed a drink in the worst way. Grabbing the nearly-empty bottle of whisky, I poured a coffee mug halfway full and took a large gulp. It burned, and I thanked the spirit of the bottle for reminding me I was alive.

Maybe you should rethink your desire to write a novel, I scolded myself. Ever since I decided to put pen to paper, my mind hadn't been the same. Maybe I wasn't cut out for it. Maybe Beth was right to tell me it was a fantasy that would never be realized.

I stumbled into the living room and fell into the soft couch.

Instinctively, my gaze turned up at the loft. That was as good a time as any for my ghostly goddess to appear.

I drank.

I stared.

I wished.

I hoped.

After close to fifteen minutes, I gave up. She was no more real than the encounter with Beth and the girls. I pinched the bridge of my nose. Nothing was right. The trip hadn't turned out like I hoped. Not yet.

Wood creaked. My eyes shot open. I tried steadying my hand so I could set the glass on the table. A horrible scratching at the door made me jump from the couch.

"Who...who's there?" My voice cracked. Blood rushed in my ears.

Another scratch, followed by several creaking steps that sounded like they came from...

My head whipped upward, and there she stood, the magnificent woman adorned in a black dress, with long, flowing hair. She smiled at me.

I felt a lump in my throat. A nervous energy ran through me like the first time I kissed a girl. I found it hard to breath. Every fiber of my being wanted her.

She looked down at me, and her plump lips curled into a smile.

I wanted to speak, but words failed me.

Her smooth skin shimmered, winking in and out.

In my stupor, I blocked out all the horrible sounds that frightened me moments before. But she turned her head toward the door, and like a curtain pulled back to reveal the horrific monster on the other side, my fears came crashing back.

Loud scratching at the door was accompanied by an almost-constant screech from outside. The aural assault surrounded me on all sides. I imagined long, deadly nails pulled down on the door outside. In my head, I could envision deep gashes in the wood. I ran my hand along my chest in a reflexive action to make sure those gashes weren't on my flesh.

The cries outside were louder, closer. My heart thundered in my chest. Blood rushed in my ears.

Then...silence. A brooding, pregnant void of sound brought more fear than relief.

"Who's out there?"

I worried I would get an answer, but none came.

What does all of this mean? The sounds? The woman? My family... why can I not find peace?

As if to answer my questions, the woman appeared again at the top of the stairs. I jumped from the couch. "Hey, hey lady...who are you?"

She didn't seem to hear my question, so I tried again. "Excuse me, but what are you doing in my cabin?"

The woman's body blinked like a flickering light, and the next moment, she was at the foot of the stairs.

I gasped, stunned by the sudden shift.

Her body winked again, and she stood inches from me.

"Fuck!" I yelled. I tried to take a step back but fell into the couch, instead. She peered down at me with dark, piercing eyes. I was frozen to the spot. There was nowhere to go, and my heart threatened to explode within me. Her face contorted and turned ugly and malevolent. She opened her mouth and screamed, but nothing came out. But I could tell she was screaming. I even felt her rancid breath pass over me, but it was silent.

Then she was gone.

Faster than what should have been possible, she disappeared. I stumbled to my feet and spun around, looking for her. I noticed my journal lying on the table; it was open. Something was written inside. I picked it up and squinted at the words.

The Lonely Cabin by Luke Bishop.

The...what? I didn't remember writing this.

A horrible screeching sound from outside startled me. I dropped the journal but then lifted it up to read while my senses were hyper-attuned to the sounds outside.

The story was weak. There were too many assumptions and not enough connecting the dots. The big reveal? It felt flat. Despite the failings, the story was my story. Something about it connected with me even though the main character, named Lex, was dead. He had been murdered by a woman named Jessie, who had long brown hair and...

What the fuck?

I dropped the journal, and when I did, the howling outside stopped.

Was my story about me?

It was impossible. I was alive, and the woman in my cabin was a ghost or something. Maybe she was my imagination.

The woman appeared out of nowhere again. Her body did that blinking/teleportation thing. It unnerved me as she flitted around the cabin in such an unnatural way and, all the while, unaware of my presence.

She reached the top of the stairs in a jarring series of bodily shifts, then disappeared.

Nothing made sense. I couldn't explain any of it. The woman. My journal. The sounds. My family. What was happening to me?

I went to get a drink to calm down, but the kitchen was bare and the whisky was gone. All that was left was a newspaper clipping, which I swore wasn't there before. The bold headline instantly caught my attention:

Man Murdered in Cabin

I swallowed hard, lifted the paper, and read.

Upon taking up residence in a rented cabin just south of Williams, Arizona, Doctor Luke Bishop was brutally murdered in a grisly act that defied logic and sanity. According to multiple sources, Dr. Bishop's body was dismembered, with parts strewn about the property with the intention that animals would devour the bits and pieces. Fourteen body parts were found, with at least another dozen unaccounted for. Unnamed sources claim they may never be found as the surrounding wildlife may have eaten them. There was no obvious motive for the slaying and no suspect. The owner of the cabin, a woman named Jessie Pittman, was herself on vacation in California at the time of the horrific murder.

Authorities ask that anyone with information about the murder please contact them immediately.

The picture accompanying the story was my cabin.

I let the paper slip from my hands and drift to the counter. This had to be a joke. I was alive! Someone was messing with me and doing a great job of breaking my mind. I couldn't stay there any longer. I had to leave immediately, before something terrible happened.

But when I went to pack my clothes, they were gone. My suitcases were missing. None of my toiletries were scattered in the bathroom like I remembered. It was as if I wasn't even there and had never been.

My heart raced as I rushed through the cabin. This had to be a mistake! I must've misplaced my things. But as time passed, my hopes faded. Finally, I fell into the couch and cupped my face in my hands. As I tried to make sense of my situation, I noticed blood running down my arms. Deep, red lines emerged on my flesh. My legs groaned in agony. Blood pooled at my feet, dark and thick. My finger fell off and thudded on the wooden floor. I jumped up, shocked at the gruesome scene, but then it vanished and everything was normal once again.

Then it dawned on me.

I had been here before.

I don't know why it took me so long for the truth to unveil itself. The trip out west. The cabin. The woman.

She had a name. Karina. She was a nurse I worked with for years. We always had a flirty relationship. About a year before Beth and I divorced, Karina and I deepened our relationship. Our last trip together before the divorce was final was to the Grand Canyon. We rented a cabin… No, we rented *this* cabin.

I looked around, and the memory of that trip came crashing back to me.

Karina and I spent hours in bed. While we slept, horrific screams startled us awake. I originally thought they were from animals outside, but they came… from Beth.

I didn't know it at the time, but Beth followed me across the country with the girls in tow, hoping to surprise me. I told her I was traveling here on a writer's retreat and would be by myself in a secluded cabin, hoping to gain inspiration. When she stood in the bedroom with the girls at her side and found me in bed with another woman, she let out a deafening cry.

I don't remember the exact details, everything turned fuzzy at that moment, but I do remember pain. Not just the physical pain of Beth's attack, but a deep, gnawing agony that seared my soul as my two girls witnessed my shame and violence. I countered Beth's rabid attack. Dark crimson blood blurred my vision. Anger and resentment and guilt fueled my brutality.

When it was over, I stood alone, covered in blood, while all I held dear or ever loved lay dead around me. I dropped to me knees and sobbed.

Wallowing in my guilt, I hadn't noticed the other person in the cabin.

It turned out Karina was married, and I hadn't known. She never spoke about it, and by the way she acted toward me, I was never tipped off. Her husband, like Beth, had followed her out west and was a few minutes too late to save her from my madness. But when he found me in that blood-filled room with her muti-lated body, and those of my wife and children, he lost his mind. And I lost my life.

But that seemed like so long ago. If I was dead, why was I still in the cabin? Why did the newspaper article never mention my family or Karina? The confusion bothered me. None of it made sense. Had I been condemned to suffer within the cabin forever?

I SANK into a soft fake-leather couch trimmed in a rough fabric. It enveloped me, though honestly, I hated those kinds of cushions. But it was the perfect place to enjoy the cabin. The chocolate-brown couch contrasted with the light oak walls and ceiling. Olive-green painted trim around the windows and doors completed the rustic ambiance.

Enjoying my morning coffee, I heard the wind blow through the pines outside. Random creaking throughout the cabin hinted at something moving, maybe the wind pushing against small boards or catching on the roof.

The otherwise silence within the cabin left me with my thoughts about the terrible last twelve months.

It started when my wife left me last year...

Brother Francis

Brother Francis slung the aged-leather bag around his shoulder. The weight of the bread inside it made the strap sink into his thick shoulder. His dark-brown woolen robe offered little protection from the leather strap, but the pain was welcomed. It reminded him of his Lord's sacrifice and the mission he was given.

The dirt path he was following took a sharp turn to the right, where it vanished amid the darkening forest. He inhaled the deep pine scent and smiled. The darkness was where he felt most alive.

The brothers back at St. Albans Monastery were expecting him soon. He left earlier that morning to secure loaves of fresh bread for their meal after vespers. The monks had not yet finished building their monastery, and the kitchen wasn't quite ready. They struck a deal with a baker in a nearby village who offered bread in exchange for prayers. The brothers of St. Albans were more than willing to make that trade.

Brother Francis was running late and had little time left before the rest of his brethren would question his absence.

He still had one errand left.

Slipping into the darkness, Brother Francis headed for the cottage he discovered on his way to the village earlier that day.

He had been to the village several times as the brothers were on a rotation to pick up the bread. But he never stumbled across the cottage before. It was so secluded it was nearly impossible to see. He only discovered it because he was following the path of a butterfly and not paying attention to where it was leading him.

Divine providence, he thought when the butterfly fluttered away, and the cottage was visible through the underbrush.

Inside was a man with thinning white hair, a rough beard, and a noticeable limp. He chased a cat out the door and shook a gnarled wooden stick at it. The cat hissed and ran into the forest.

Brother Francis crouched low and waited. He looked to either side of the cottage for visitors and figured the old man was hidden in the forest for a reason. Brother Francis licked his lips and ran his hand along the dull metal knife hidden under his robe. *I must remember this place*, he thought. *Sin lives here.* He carefully retreated from the cottage and headed for the village. His pace was quick because the sooner he gathered the bread, the sooner he would be back to the old man.

◆

"GET OUT OF HERE, you evil creature!" the old man yelled.

Brother Francis gulped the cool air. His heart thudded in his chest.

I've been discovered, he thought. But then with the faint flicker of a candle inside the cottage, he noticed the silhouette of the cat scurrying away from the old man's foot. Brother Francis wiped the sweat from his brow and took a few calming breaths. *It was the cat, not me.*

Waiting for the man to go back inside, Brother Francis silently crept toward the cottage. He ran a hand along his knife and felt a tingle within his loins. He said a prayer for forgiveness, then opened the door.

The old man hobbled up from his wooden chair and clung to a wooden stick for support. A fire blazed in a stone fireplace behind him, a black cauldron hanging over it with water inside.

"What are you doing in here? Nobody said you could come in!" The old man's eyes widened and his arm shook. The dingy tunic he wore over woolen breeches hung loosely on his gaunt frame. The fuzzy white hair on his head was disheveled, and his scraggly gray beard was streaked with white. The man had lived long enough to accumulate sin. It was Brother Francis's mission to expunge it from the earth.

A grin snaked across Brother Francis's pudgy face. "The Lord led me here," he said in a dark, deep voice. "I must never turn my back on His will."

The old man scrunched his face in confusion, a look Brother Francis saw often. Many sinners didn't understand why he was the chosen vessel of vengeance. They would find out in the next life.

"I don't care what your Lord says," the old man said.

"But I do."

▲

EVER SINCE HE WAS A BOY, Brother Francis, or just Francis as he was called then, had known he was God's chosen instrument. When the Danes attacked his homestead and murdered his family, they left his mother as a bloodied mess in the center of their small home. He was only seven at the time, but the image of his mother with her chest split open and her lungs flung over her shoulders made her look like a gory, red angel. He took it as a sign. It was God speaking to him.

Sin has tainted those around you. Punish the sin and live.

The words penetrated his young mind, and he had no doubt it was God's voice. Who was he to ignore the calling?

The Danes left him alive, alone and desperate. A small group of monks discovered the destroyed homestead, and when they found him hiding underneath the smoldering remains of the house, a bone in his hand, they took pity on him and had him join them. He had been part of their brotherhood ever since.

THE OLD MAN could barely stand. His body convulsed, and Brother Francis could tell the man concentrated hard to remain upright. Then he pulled the knife from under his robe.

The dull blade was as long as his hand. He had found it near an old Roman settlement that had been overgrown for centuries. The handle, that part was personal.

When he felt the call of God while staring at his mother's bloody corpse, Francis was compelled by the Spirit to claim a piece of his mother. Her arm was shattered, and a thick bone penetrated her flesh. He snapped it off and held tightly to it. When the monks found him, that was what he held in his hand. He refused to give it up. Later, when he found the Roman blade, he fashioned a knife with the bone as its handle. It became the tool he used to exact the Lord's vengeance on sin.

Brother Francis turned the knife over in his hand.

The old man's eyes widened even more. Wood snapped and crackled in the fireplace.

"There's no need for that, Brother," the old man said.

"I'm afraid it's what I was called to do. The Lord cannot stand sin. He's given me a mission. Sin must be dealt with."

The old man held up his hands, pleading. "I don't harm any souls. I'm not a bad person."

"All are evil and must repent." Brother Francis pointed the knife at him. "Are you prepared to atone for your sins?"

The old man nodded vigorously. "Yes, I'll do whatever you want."

Brother Francis lunged at him, and the old man shouted.

The first time Francis blotted out someone's sin, he prayed for days afterward. The guilt weighed heavily on him, but he was only ten. He hadn't fully understood the necessity of his actions then.

At a tavern in a small village, a woman approached the brothers and offered sexual favors for their blessing and a bite of food. She danced around the monks with her breasts exposed. The brothers, there were six of them at the time, shunned the woman and decried her lascivious behavior. But Francis was intrigued, watching as she repeated the same actions with the other patrons. The tavern owner tossed her out.

Later that night, as they left the tavern to retreat for the night at the inn, Francis saw her huddled in an alley behind the tavern, the glow of the moon barely reaching her.

When the brothers had all gone to bed, he snuck out of the room and headed for the woman.

Luckily, she was there.

He stood over her, watching her sleep. Her breasts were still exposed, and they rose gently with each breath. Visions of his mother flashed in his mind.

The brothers instilled in him the notion that the reason his family was killed by the Danes was they had succumbed to sin. The Danes were sent to punish them, and the only reason Francis survived was his innocence.

Like his mother, this woman was a sinner and needed to pay.

Francis picked up a sharp rock that lay near her foot. It was the size of his fist and angular. With his mother's bloody body dominating his thoughts, he fell to the woman...and cut.

♦

Brother Francis plunged the Roman blade into the old man's stomach. Blood gushed out, and the man screamed. His cries were heavenly, the song of angels. It was what sin sounded like when it escaped the body.

"Please, no," the old man said. He was frail and unable to stop Brother Francis's terrible attack.

The two men fell to the dirt floor. The old man's screams were silenced when the breath in his lungs was forced out from the fall.

"Sin will never win!" Brother Francis screamed. He continued to brutalize the old man with the bone-handled knife. Blood splashed on his face. A sharp tang was followed by the stench of offal.

"I repent," the old man whispered. His eyes rolled back in his head.

But to Brother Francis, it wasn't enough. The Lord demanded more. He leaned back on his haunches and stared down at the bloody sinner. Then he sliced open the man's tunic, exposing his torn stomach.

"Blood must be spilled, a sacrifice of atonement."

Brother Francis grabbed the knife with both hands, then slammed it into the man's stomach. The blade sank into a bloodied mess of flesh and intestines. It clung to his hands like thick mud. Brother Francis pulled his knife free and said a quick prayer. The next part was the worst, but it was the most necessary.

He sliced along the man's chest, going from just below his neck all the way to his stomach. Blood streaked down either side of the large gash. He sawed through the cartilage at the front of the ribs. Sweat beaded on his forehead. The dull knife got stuck when he tried slicing through the second connecting piece. He struggled to break through. Praying for guidance, he finally broke the bond.

The old man groaned.

Brother Francis wiped the sweat from his cheeks, smearing the old man's blood on his face. A sharp tang invaded his nostrils. He held up one of his hands; the old man's sin coated his pale flesh in dark crimson. Slowly, he extended his tongue and licked. He had never done that before, but the blood seemed so…inviting.

It tasted like the warm butter Brother Marcus made in the monastery, but tainted.

Brother Francis spit it out and wiped his tongue on his sleeve. "Sin cannot enter my body," he grumbled.

The old man barely breathed. Blood spilled out from his gaping wound.

Brother Francis said a quick prayer and continued to extract sin from the old man.

WHEN FRANCIS WAS thirteen years old, he was sent to help the poor in a nearby village. Left alone with only a brown robe to signify his affiliation, he wandered the village looking for someone to help.

He spotted an old woman wearing dirty rags and barefoot behind the butcher's shop, digging through bones and rotten flesh. She was fighting with wild dogs for the scraps.

Francis slipped his bone-handled knife out from under his robe and approached the woman.

"Can I help?" he asked.

His voice startled her, and she whipped her head around, staring at him with large bloodshot eyes. A vein pulsed on her pale forehead. Dirt and blood caked her cheeks. She was missing most of her teeth, and grimy hair that reached her shoulders hung loosely from her scalp.

"You come here to steal my food," she snarled, pointing at him with a bony finger.

Francis had been warned of witches in the area, and he wondered if she was one. "I've come to help. It's my duty."

"All you religious folk are nothing but liars. You don't know the truth of the old ways."

Her words sent a shiver down his spine. Francis knew without a doubt she was a witch. If not a witch, then at least a heathen that needed God. Images of his mother flashed in his mind. *Sin must be dealt with*, a dark voice said in his head. He knew what to do.

Chasing the famished dogs from the stinking pile of animal scraps, he attacked the old woman. She was too slow to react, and with his full weight bearing down on her, he shoved the knife into her belly. The old hag screamed, and he cuffed her.

"You will repent!"

Blood spilled over his hand. Francis twisted the blade, feeling her soft insides giving resistance. Then he sliced sideways and ripped open a massive wound.

The old woman clutched at his hands, her eyes going impossibly wide. Her mouth opened to scream, but no sound came out.

"Your soul will be free," he whispered. With a final cut, he widened the wound so her stomach spilled out, no doubt filled with the maggot-infested meat she had been devouring moments earlier.

"You're free now. Go to the Lord and embrace the truth."

▮

BROTHER FRANCIS LOOKED DOWN at the old man who stubbornly clung to life. Those that needed cleansing the most were the ones unwilling to accept it.

Closing his eyes and envisioning the angelic forces at his side, Brother Francis turned his gaze back to the old man. Setting his knife to the side, he grabbed the man's ribs with both hands, then pulled them open.

The man screamed as bones snapped. Blood spilled out all around him. Underneath the ribs, coated in blood, were two large white sacks.

Brother Francis caressed the left one with both hands, feeling it inflate slightly as the old man clung to his sin. Shaking his head, Brother Francis ripped the man's lung from his chest and tossed it over the man's shoulder where it splatted on the dirt. Blood splashed outward, creating the visual of a crimson wing.

The man cried out and exhaled his last breath.

Grabbing the other lung, Brother Francis repeated the step, hoisting the man's lung from his chest and letting it crash to the ground. An open cavity, filling fast with blood and smelling like shit, was all that was left.

The cat returned and bit into the man's intestines. Brother Francis thought to scare it off but then remembered how the man had treated it, so left the cat to take its portion.

The old man's carcass lay on the floor in a grotesque mockery of an angel. The Danes had taught Brother Francis the ways of God. Those lessons burned in his brain and fueled him to follow the commands he was given.

Brother Francis bowed his head and prayed for the man's soul. His sin was purged, and his body was offered as a sacrifice. It was all Brother Francis could do for the man's salvation. The rest was up to the man. And God.

Pushing himself off the floor, Brother Francis looked down at the man. He wondered if at that moment the man was speaking with God. He hoped so. He hoped all the people whose souls he cleansed had done so.

Before leaving the home, Brother Francis cleaned his face, hands, and his robe with the water in the pot over the fire. Some of the blood was stubborn and refused to go, but he knew by the time he got back to the monastery, it would dry enough to not be seen on the darkly-colored fabric. They hadn't noticed it before.

Brother Francis grabbed the bread and left the house.

As he navigated his way through the dark forest, he softly sang hymns and offered up prayers for the soul of the old man. Brother Francis had done his duty, and the rest of the brothers would rest easy, with bellies full of bread. Sin didn't belong in the world, and Brother Francis was more than willing to do his part to get rid of it. One sinner at a time.

Two Deaths,
One Wife

The soul-crushing grief of losing my wife the first time nearly broke me. The second time shattered what remained.

I was hiding in the basement with my back to the wall. Rancid water splashed against my boot. I guessed it had been like this since the dead rose from the ground three years ago. My wife Lexi and I moved into the house after the previous occupants were mauled by a pack of dead. We tried to help them, but the dead overwhelmed us and it was all I could do to get the two of us to safety.

"What's that?" I remember asking Lexi after the skirmish.

We ran far from the dead, and when we rested, she sat on a curb, pulling her arm to herself. Dark crimson stained her olive-drab military coat. When she looked up at me with her sky-blue eyes, I knew it was bad.

"I got bit," she whispered.

I covered my mouth with a hand. "No," I breathed.

"I'm sorry, James. I thought I was careful."

I sat and wrapped my arms around her. I choked up as she sobbed until the sun went down.

That night, we took over the house. As the night wore on and the realization of what was to come sank in, we made love for hours.

The turn occurred in the morning. She died as the sun rose and the birds sang.

My heart burst as she took her last breath. A few moments of horrific silence followed. It was broken by a wet gasp as life returned. Her eyes shot open and were already a dark, milky color. She thrashed on the bed. I should've killed her then, but sentimentality and love prevented me from acting. How could I put a bullet in her head?

Lexi growled and snarled. She clawed at me, but I jumped from the bed and stumbled backward. I grabbed my cargo pants and military jacket, blew a kiss at my growling bride, and left.

But I didn't go far. I couldn't leave her. She was my everything. My heart belonged to her, and I lost the nerve to do what should've been done.

I stayed close to her when she shuffled out of the house, tracking her every movement. When two punks tried to trap her for their amusement, I chased them off.

"Get the fuck out of here!" I shouted, waving my gun like a madman.

"What's wrong with you, douche? She's dead!" one of them said.

"If you value your own lives, I suggest you move on. She's mine."

"Claiming the dead? Dude, are you gonna fuck her?" the other one said. I lost my cool and shot him in the leg.

He fell screaming, and his friend shouted at me, calling me a lunatic. Lexi devoured the injured man, and his friend ran away yelling he would get revenge.

I stood in awe watching my dear bride shove flesh and muscle into her mouth. At some point in the feast, my brain snapped.

What the hell had I done? She was dead. Lexi was gone forever.

But still I couldn't put her down.

I regretted that decision.

THE DANK BASEMENT mirrored my soul: blackened and sour. I was hiding from Lexi.

My wife, or what was left of her, shambled across the floor above me. I made the mistake of trailing too closely to her and she caught my scent. I couldn't shake her no matter what because I refused to get too far away. I knew she was dead, but it was Lexi! I cursed myself again as she shuffled closer to the basement door.

I moved my foot, and the water splashed.

Lexi stopped. I prayed she hadn't heard me, but my prayers fell on deaf ears. The basement door smashed open, and Lexi groaned, sniffing the air like a dog and taking a step.

In her dead state, she lacked the ability to navigate the stairs, and she tumbled forward and crashed into the water next to me.

"Lexi, it's me!" I shouted.

She growled and snarled, snatching my leg and trying to bite me.

"No, Lexi, please!" I yanked my leg away and stumbled backward.

Her arm was broken from the fall, and a bone jutted from her decaying skin making her grasp weak. She sniffed and lunged toward me.

Instinctively, I fired my pistol, and the bullet blasted a hole in her head. Black brains sprayed in the air. She fell at my feet, into the water. Her decaying body lay still as I waited for her to get up. I breathed heavily, and guilt blossomed inside me. What had I done?

I dropped to my knees and cradled her head in my lap. Tears ran down my cheeks, and I couldn't stop them, not that I would. I felt her death all over again. It was like a finality settled in that hadn't been there before.

Thick blood spilled out from her wound and coated my pants. I cried for hours knowing she was never coming back.

When I cried my last, I found plastic sheeting and covered her. I slowly walked up the steps. When I reached the top, I turned around and wiped the remaining tears off my face.

"Goodbye, my love. I'll never forget."

When I left the house, a small herd of dead was chasing a young boy down the street. Anger burned bright inside. I wanted them all dead for taking Lexi. With nothing left to hold me back, I raced after the dead with a burning rage, ready to unleash my fury on the monsters that stole my wife.

Necrotic Sanitation

Author's note: this was written for a gross out contest. You have been warned.

I PULLED THE TAMPON OUT OF THE TRASH. WRAPPED IN TOILET paper, it was spotted in a dark crimson that was nearly brown and had a pungent bouquet. It was still wet. I unwrapped it and inhaled it like a Cuban cigar, imagining what it must have been like to be inside of the woman, filling with her essence. Droplets of blood tickled inside my nostrils.

My dick grew stiff in my pants.

"Damn it, John, hurry up in there. I need a cigarette bad," my co-worker, Dave, said into the open restroom door. I shoved the moist tampon into my pocket, patting the treasure to make sure it was secure, and hurriedly finished cleaning the bathroom.

When I was done, I carried my tools in a small bucket and left the bathroom.

"About fucking time. What the hell were you doing in there,

pounding your pud?" Dave asked. After smoking three cigarettes, Dave had finally come back inside the building. He had to be at least ten years older than me and lorded his superiority like a man covering up the fact his dick is two inches long when hard.

"Some lady left shit all over the seat. Blood too. Some of it had crusted and wouldn't come off." I didn't lie. One of the stalls looked like it had been destroyed. I kinda hoped it was the woman whose tampon I carried in my pocket.

Dave wrinkled his nose in disgust. We were the overnight care-takers at the Winthrop office building down on Delmar Avenue. Dave had been here for fifteen years; I had been here for four. The job sucked except for the opportunity to uncover keepsakes like the one soaking through my pocket. I could feel the cold blood on my leg. I had no idea whose it could've been. We hadn't seen anyone all night.

The morning shift would be there in thirty minutes, and I couldn't wait. I reached my hand in my pocket to gently stroke the used tampon. I pulled my hand out and, on the sly, brought my hand to my nose and sniffed. Fuck, it was amazing!

"Smelling your dick?" Dave asked.

I smiled. "Nope, just your mom's cooch."

"Fucking gross. You know I came out of that vag, right?"

"And I came in it," I replied.

"You're sick, John. Go home, man. I've got this until the morning crew shows up."

He didn't have to tell me twice. I had a date, and it was seeping in my pocket.

WHEN I GOT HOME, the odor of Dave's mom filled the air. She had been dead for months, just how I liked 'em.

"Martha, I got you something," I said to the silent house. I imagined her sweet reply of, "What is it, dear?"

"Another gift," I said. I patted the tampon in my pocket and headed to the bedroom. When I opened the door, there was no denying Martha was there. Her alluring scent was strong. I clicked on the light and gasped in wonder.

There, on my bed, was the decayed corpse of Martha, spread eagle in her birthday suit. Four other tampons were shoved into her rotten pussy. I pulled the one from my pocket, licking it and savoring the tang.

"Here you go, Martha. To fill you up." I leaned closer and peered into the dark abyss that was her vagina. I moved two of the tampons out of the way and inserted the fresh one. A small worm escaped from inside her and slithered under her body.

"That's my girl," I cooed. The erection in my pants stiffened to the point where it ached. What I wouldn't do to see Dave's face right then!

Martha waited patiently. Expectantly.

How could I deny her any longer?

I unzipped my pants and stepped out of them. I moved between her legs and pulled one of the older tampons out of her to make room. Maggots crawled all over it. A couple of them dropped to the bed between her legs. I shoved the decayed tampon in my mouth. Maggots burst like pop rocks when I bit down on them. The dried blood barely tasted like blood anymore, which was why the new tampon was so needed.

With the string hanging out of my mouth, I held myself poised just outside of her waiting vagina. Then I slipped myself inside.

She was dry, but the tampons offered relief. Something wriggled inside, and the movement sent me into overdrive. I thrust harder and harder. Flesh on her abdomen split open, and white worms squirmed out. I couldn't stop. It was sheer ecstasy! I bit down on the tampon to quell my growing excitement. If I wasn't careful, I would go too soon.

Minutes later, I exploded inside of her like I had done nearly every day since she died. I groaned loudly and stayed inside her until I gave her my very last drop. When I finally pulled out, the tampons had done their job and kept my semen inside her.

I absently nibbled on the tampon in my mouth and smiled. All I could think of was how funny it was that I told Dave what I did earlier. I wondered if he would find the humor in it too.

Peace Comes from Blood

When I was eight, my mom gave me what she thought was the greatest Christmas present: a brown teddy bear. Don't get me wrong, bears are cool and all, but the best gift? I didn't even think so when I was a kid! What she gave me instead was a curse.

To this day, Mr. Giggles lives with me.

He needs blood. Always more blood. If I refuse? He takes mine, but I have no more to give. So I kill for him. I kill for me. Mr. Giggles needs his food, and I need peace. Peace comes from blood.

Milk and Cookies

Santa demands milk and cookies, so children leave them out. One year, a child forgot to leave the offering and lost her head. Since that horrible night, newspapers and news stations send out alerts three weeks before Christmas:

Make Sure To Leave Out The Milk And Cookies!

Parents assure their children are safe by guarding the milk and cookies until Santa leaves, protecting their children from a horrific end. He winks and nods and gobbles the treat, then up the chimney he goes, seeking the child who refuses to share.

Some nights, the terrible screams are heard throughout the night.

CHRISTMAS STALKINGS

WHEN I HUNG THE STOCKINGS ALONG THE MANTLE, I WAS REMINDED of a powerful dream I had. In my dream, bloody bodies swung in the forest, hanging by ropes around their necks.

They were the ghoulish remains of those I killed.

The bodies were male and female, both young and old. They surrounded me and groaned, seeking freedom from their captivity. I couldn't let them have that.

When I woke in a cold sweat, I knew what had to be done. I needed to kill again and then hang the bodies like my Christmas stockings as a gift to myself.

LITTLE DEVILS

BEN OPENED THE FADED WOODEN DOOR TO HIS FAMILY'S CABIN. IT creaked on rusty hinges. A musty odor wafted outward. He turned to his wife, Mindy, and gave a sheepish grin.

"It was in better shape the last time I was here," he said.

Snow swirled around them in the twilight, large flakes blowing into the darkened cabin. Ben shivered.

Mindy looked down at their five-year-old son, Justin, who was holding his crotch and dancing from one foot to the other.

"Can we at least get the lights on so Justin can pee? I don't think the poor kid can handle waiting much longer."

Ben ruffled his son's curly brown hair. "I'll see what I can do. If nothing else, he can go outside. It's what boys do."

Mindy narrowed her eyes at him, a look that questioned his sanity and that he saw often.

"Or there's an outhouse out back," he added.

Even in the evening darkness, Ben could see Mindy rolling her eyes. She was adamant there was no way in hell she would use an outhouse. What century were they living in? When he suggested they go to the cabin for Christmas, he convinced her his dad installed a working toilet inside and they should be fine. He hadn't personally used it, since he hadn't been to the cabin for over fifteen years, but he expected the upgrades to the place to be a welcome addition.

Ben clicked on the flashlight on his phone and bathed the darkness inside in a circle of light.

"Yuck," Justin said.

"You said it," Mindy said.

"Yeah, I don't remember it being like this," Ben said. He had been so filled with nostalgic memories that he hadn't anticipated what the place would be like after years of neglect. He assumed there would be some amount of dust and stale air, but what greeted them was something else.

Cobwebs stretched across the great room in front of them. Attached to the ceiling and stretching toward the walls, the cascading webs made it feel more like Halloween than Christmas.

Ben let out a heavy sigh. "I'm sorry, Min, I didn't think it would be this bad."

"Pee!" Justin said, his feet shuffling like an agitated bull ready to attack.

Mindy shot Ben a questioning look, which snapped him out of his stupor. "The bathroom should be straight ahead. Dad said it was across the hall from the bedroom there," he said, pointing to the short hallway directly in front of them.

Mindy placed a hand on Justin's back and guided him toward the hall, pulling out her phone and turning on the light. When they got to the bathroom door, she pushed it open and they stepped inside.

"Oh, gross," Justin said. Ben couldn't see what it was, but considering the state of the place, he could imagine it was something bad.

"Don't worry about it. Just go, or we can go outside," Mindy said. It took a moment, but he soon heard the splash of his son finally relieving himself.

Ben stepped into the main room of the cabin. It was a giant square, with the kitchen flanking the door to his right, a dining table in front of him to his left, and a living room area on the far-right side of the room. Above the kitchen and the living room were two lofts. There used to be two beds per loft, though he had no idea if that was still the case.

His family built the cabin sixty years earlier on a piece of land in central Michigan, sort of at the first knuckle of the middle finger if you were looking at the state like a hand. It was a beautiful land, filled with pine trees and snowmobile trails. A nearby river used to be the only way to bathe when he was a kid, though Ben's dad had running water installed by the time he turned ten. His dad often said the cost of the land was far too high but never did share what he paid for it.

Despite the possibility of snowstorms, his family always stayed at the cabin over Christmas, until the year Ben's mom died. He was fourteen when she passed, the cancer devouring her from the inside.

It was the one Christmas he hadn't gone with his parents to the cabin. A good friend of his invited him to his family's ski trip to Colorado, and while out there, he received a call his mother passed while at the cabin. Apparently, her body was so damaged by the cancer they couldn't even have an open-casket funeral. Ben regretted missing that trip ever since and vowed to recreate those moments with his own family.

Standing inside the building, the memories of the place exposed long-dormant feelings that overwhelmed him. A dark, unsettling sadness crept over him, nothing like the glee he expected when convincing his family to reignite his old family tradition of staying at the cabin over Christmas.

"It didn't flush," Mindy said.

Ben was ripped from his thoughts. "Sorry. What did you say?" he asked.

"The toilet didn't flush. We're gonna need to figure it out, because Justin did more than just pee."

The little boy beamed at his dad. "If it's brown, flush it down," he said, then giggled to himself.

The potty humor was what Ben needed to break the tension and relax.

"Ok, ok. I'll figure it out." He laughed and shook his head.

"Have you figured out the lights yet?" Mindy asked. She walked past him and flipped the light switch. Nothing happened.

"Oh, the breakers," Ben said. He went to the closet on his left and pulled it open. Dusting off the black metal box, he opened the door and flipped on the main breaker. A radio burst to life with the sounds of an old country song. Mindy yelped, and Justin jumped. Ben's heart raced.

"Sorry!" he said, as though he had anything to do with it. "I guess the power works." Light illuminated the cabin. Ben found the radio and clicked it off.

"I don't think the power is gonna help get rid of the creepy vibes of this place," Mindy said when he rejoined them.

"Nothing a little cleaning can't take care of. Why don't you two see if the tv still works, and I'll get rid of the spiderwebs." Mindy turned to leave, and Ben grabbed her arm, pulling her close. "Thank you for this," he said softly. "It means a lot to me." He kissed her soft lips.

"Yuck!" Justin said, making them both laugh.

Ben found a broom and some towels and got to work ridding the place of years of neglect. By the time he was done, Mindy had started a fire in the wood burning stove in the living room, and she and Justin settled in on the blue couch, watching a black and white movie.

Listening to the voices coming from the tv, Ben realized it was *It's a Wonderful Life*. It warmed his heart. Every year, his family would gather together to watch that old movie right here in the cabin. How fortunate was it that he could do that with his own family?

"Good thing the tv works. Otherwise, we'd have been screwed," Ben said as he joined his family. The movie was nearly halfway over. When he sat next to Justin, a small puff of dust burst from the couch.

"I think something's wrong with the tv. It's not in color," Justin said.

Ben smiled. "It's how they used to be, before my time. Color was a special treat for some people. At least that's what I hear. Besides, this movie is in black and white anyway."

"Who still has a tv like that? This place hasn't had visitors in years, has it?" Mindy asked.

"I don't think so. Dad told me he'd come up here every year, but I'm wondering if he was lying to me. It had to have taken years for those spiders to make webs that large."

"That seems like an odd thing to lie about."

"Beats me. Maybe it was so I wouldn't worry about him being alone after mom died."

Mindy turned back to the movie. Until it was over, the three of them sat huddled close together, the fire crackling and casting a warm glow on them. When the credits rolled, Ben realized Justin had fallen asleep, his head leaning against Mindy. He stared at the two of them, the loves of his life, and was thankful to be there with them at that moment.

"What?" Mindy asked when she caught him gazing at them.

"Just realizing how lucky I am. Come on, let's get Justin to bed. Maybe we can break in the cabin the right way." Ben winked, and a grin plastered on his face.

Mindy shook her head and giggled softly, trying to not wake up Justin.

"Just help me get him to bed first, and then we'll see."

"We can let him use the bedroom downstairs tonight, and we can take one of the lofts. I'd hate for him to wake up in the middle of the night and stumble down the steps. They're pretty steep."

His family wasn't from the construction field, and they didn't bring in anyone to inspect their work. The stairs leading up to the lofts was built from thick logs and were at such an impossibly-high incline that the handrail was a necessity, not an afterthought.

They tucked Justin in bed and left his door open. As it was directly across from the loft upstairs, they would have a perfect view toward his room if he needed anything.

"Come on, let's play upstairs," Ben said with the same mischievous smile on his face.

"Ben Lynch, you never give up, do you?" Mindy kissed him and sauntered toward the stairs, taking each one slowly as she ascended to the loft.

I

IT WAS close to three in the morning when Ben was shaken awake from his postcoital slumber. He and Mindy enjoyed themselves earlier, and both passed out soon after.

"What the hell?" he said, rubbing sleep from his eyes. A sound like faint whispers surrounded him, and he couldn't place the source of it. "Justin? Is that you?"

Moonlight streamed in from the small window at the back end of the loft. It cast a yellow shadow on the floor, illuminating dust mites and other particles drifting in the air.

The whispers continued, and Ben whipped his head all around, the hairs on his neck stiffening. His heart beat faster, and the drowsiness was chased away by the adrenaline coursing through him.

"Justin?"

He jumped from bed, the movement enough to make Mindy shift. But when he did, he hit his head on an exposed log from the low, sloping ceiling.

"Oh, shit!" he said. He was loud enough to wake Mindy, who sat up with the sheet held close to her chest.

"What is it?" she asked, her words coming as a soft mist in the chilly air.

"I thought I heard something."

"Is it Justin?"

Ben shook his head. "I don't think so. It was like people were whispering."

Mindy brought the sheet up higher, wrapping her arms around herself. "Are you serious? Who would be out here at this time of night?"

"That's what scared me. But I don't hear them anymore."

"Go check on Justin. Make sure he's ok," Mindy said.

"Yeah, sure thing."

The creepiness was fading from Ben, especially after Mindy turned on the table lamp. He tossed on his pajamas and a t-shirt, then climbed down the stairs.

When he poked his head into Justin's room, he spoke softly. "Hey, son, are you ok in here? Nothing to be afraid of, is there?" He squinted at the bundle on the bed. Justin didn't move and was eerily quiet. "Justin?"

Ben moved closer and reached out to touch the lump. It collapsed on itself. It was nothing but a blanket. Justin was gone.

"What the hell?" he yelled out. Flicking on the light, he ripped the sheet and blanket off the bed, only to confirm his fears. Justin wasn't there.

"Mindy! He's not here!"

He heard a thud as she bolted out of bed. In a mad scramble, she dressed and rushed down the stairs.

"Where is he?" she asked, her voice trembling.

"I don't know. Hurry, we need to check the cabin."

Ben scrambled to the other loft and found it empty. They searched under very piece of furniture and in every crevice, but when they were done, he was still missing.

"The outhouse!" Ben said, hoping his son had explored outside. "He's got to be there." He raced out the back door, following footsteps in the snow to the small red shack. He flung the door open.

"Justin? Are you in here?"

His voice echoed in the small building. The electric heater that had been left out there for cold nights was on, creating a warm and inviting atmosphere.

Something bubbled in the toilet. Fearing his son had fallen in, Ben lifted the plastic lid and gasped.

About six feet below the toilet seat was a thick, murky slurry of age-old piss and shit. But that wasn't what startled him. It was sight of his son, wrapped in a white-and-red-stripped bubble, beating against the inside. Tears streamed down Justin's face. The translucent cocoon wobbled in the thick substance with every move he made.

"Justin!" Ben screamed. The bizarre vision unsettled him, his thoughts swirling about how to remove him from the mess.

Mindy peered over his shoulder. "Oh my god!" She covered her mouth with her hand. "Ben, you need to get him out of there!"

Ben couldn't think. His mind had gone blank, as though someone had wiped it clean. He was staring at a nightmare that froze him to the core.

Mindy shook him. "Damn it, Ben. Do something!"

She broke his trance, and he snapped back to reality. Though it made no sense, his son was now floating in a pit of human waste, trapped within some kind of candy-like bubble.

"Yeah, ok, ok. I need a stick or something. I gotta break him out."

"You can't do that! What if he drowns?"

He reluctantly turned from Justin to face her. "Then what would you have me do?" he snarled.

"I don't know. Go down there?"

"Did you see what it is?"

"Fine, if you won't, then I will." Mindy shoved him aside, but he quickly regained his position.

"No. You stay here. I'll do it."

Something stirred in the liquid below, and both of them turned to face their son. Next to his candy-cane-looking prison, two of the meanest-looking elves flanked him. Their heads were bulbous, and pointy ears stuck out from underneath tattered felt caps. They smiled up at them, thin, red lips pulled back, exposing rows of sharp teeth.

"Yes," one of them said in a rough, deep voice, "please come down. We are owed our share."

"What the hell?" Mindy yelled. "Ben, what are those things?"

Words caught in his throat. Had anyone told him elves were real, he would've thought they were crazy. His mind was either playing a nasty trick on him, or they did indeed exist and they had his son. He couldn't imagine what they planned to do to him.

"Leave him alone!" Ben said to the elves bobbing in the awful liquid.

"Or what?" one of them replied. It placed a hand on Justin's cocoon and tapped long, gnarled fingers on the hard shell. "He'll be a tasty treat, much like your mother." It cackled, and Ben's eyes sprang wide.

His mother? How did that thing know about his mom?

"Ben, you have to get Justin out of there!" Mindy said. He felt her quivering hand on his shoulder.

"Enjoy your holiday," the other elf said. Then the two of them pushed down on the translucent orb surrounding Justin, forcing him below the surface of the muck.

Justin beat against the inside, screaming for help.

Ben reacted by instinct and dropped feetfirst through the toilet, passing stains left by years of use, and landed in the cold slurry. He was assaulted by the stench of human waste as it splashed on his face and arms.

The elves screamed and clawed at him. Hot streaks ran across his arms as they attacked. They were relentless, but he was determined. Ben backhanded one of them and knocked it several feet away.

In the dim light penetrating through the toilet above, he realized they were in a massive cavern that stretched out all around for at least fifty feet. He didn't have time to process it as the second elf lunged at him.

The elf clung to his Ben's head and wildly clawed at him, like a wolverine tearing into its victim. Ben screamed and tried to protect himself, thinking only about Justin and rescuing him from these evil things.

Ben grabbed the elf, it was only about two feet tall, and the thing clawed at his face. One of its nails dug into Ben's cheek and ripped open a wound that stretched from his mouth to his eye. Ben screamed, but fueled by fury, he clutched the elf and flung it into the abyss. It landed with a splash.

Burning pain raced across Ben's face. Blood poured out of the wound. His tongue poked out of the tear in his cheek, igniting a shock of pain.

The two elves grumbled but swam toward him, snarling and hurling curse words at him.

Breaking through the pain, Ben focused again on Justin. He needed to save his son.

He pushed the hard candy bubble away from the elves and punched it. The shell held. He punched it again.

Inside the thing, Justin flailed and cried hysterically.

"I'll get you, son, don't worry," Ben said. He punched and punched, his knuckles bleeding and leaving red streaks on the shell. The elves climbed on his back, laughing and shredding his flesh with their wicked claws.

"We'll taste blood, one way or the other," one of the elves snarled. One of them bit into Ben's shoulder, ripping its head back and tearing his flesh with it. Ben cried out.

Above them, Mindy was throwing sticks and anything else she could get her hands on. "Get off of him!" she screamed.

Ben's anger grew fierce. The elves were relentless in their attack, which ignited his determination to free his son.

With one last punch, he broke through the candy shell. Justin screamed when one of the elves launched off his dad and landed on him.

Ben's determination overpowered his failing strength, and he grabbed hold of the elf attacking Justin and tossed it into the darkness, where it splashed into the filth. He grabbed the other elf attacking him in a chokehold, and wrapping one hand across its forehead, he twisted until the neck snapped in a sickening crunch. The elf went limp in his hands, and he tossed it across the cavern.

Justin's tears streamed down his face while he bobbed in the liquid waste.

"I got ya, buddy, hold on," Ben said, grinding his teeth against the pain. He lifted Justin out of the muck, thick strands of gross water dripping off him.

"Hand him up," Mindy said. Ben lifted him higher until he felt Justin's weight pulled upward by Mindy.

A hand splashed into the water, and Ben whipped his head toward the remaining elf.

"Blood will be spilt. This isn't over yet," the elf said, then dove into the water.

Ben waited, anxiously turning from side to side expecting a

surprise attack. The elf never resurfaced. Instead of waiting for it, he climbed out of the sewage, through the toilet, and into the cold night.

MONTHS AFTER THE INCIDENT, Ben sold the cabin and the surrounding property to a developer who had grand plans for a wilderness retreat. He didn't disclose the incident, and with Mindy's urging, closed the deal at a less-than-fair market price. It was off his hands; the nightmare was over.

Before he signed the papers, he made one last trip to the cabin. It was his way of creating closure to the events that happened over Christmas.

He dug through the cabin, looking for any clue as to why there were elves in the outhouse, an absurd thought but one he knew was deadly.

In the main bedroom downstairs, he discovered a notepad with his father's handwriting on it. Inside were mostly phone numbers of local services and of family members. There was one page that made his heart leap into his throat.

Near the back of the notebook, he found the word Elf scribbled. Below that was the name and phone number of a man named Albert Durgin, with the word Plumber next to it. Ben assumed that was whoever his dad called to get the water running in the cabin. Had he discovered the wicked things in the outhouse? Ben set the notebook down and stared blankly at the wall, replaying the events in his head, the ones he tried desperately to forget. If his dad had known, why didn't he say anything? He wondered when his dad found out. Maybe it was after his mom died.

The thought struck him like a lightning bolt. His mom. Her funeral was closed casket. She had died at the cabin with only his dad around. Did the elves get her? Was his dad covering it up?

Ben shivered. There was evil nearby, and he wanted no part in it. Whatever the real reason for his mom's death, he chose to believe it was the cancer and not some diminutive devils.

A random memory came back with a vengeance: his dad complaining about the cost of the land. Had he made a deal that carried with it horrific consequences? He didn't want to believe his father would willingly put his family in danger all for a piece of property.

He left the cabin, but not before burning the notebook in the wood-burning stove. If he hadn't already signed the papers to sell it, he briefly considered lighting the whole place up.

THE FOLLOWING CHRISTMAS, he couldn't help but think about the horror of the year before. Not once did Justin or Mindy bring up the cabin and the events with the wicked elves. He was thankful for that, though it never left his mind. Instead of trying to recreate the traditions of his childhood, Ben was content to create something new with his family; to build new memories he hoped Justin would someday try to create with his family.

On Christmas Eve, Ben and Mindy tucked Justin into bed.

"Tomorrow we'll see what Santa brought you," Ben said. "What's the one thing you hope he brings?"

Justin smiled at his parents, a wide gap in his front teeth where his most recent tooth had fallen out. "A new video game," he said. His bright, cheerful face showed no hint of the tragedy from a year ago. Ben was thankful for the boy's ability to move on from the horror.

"We'll see about that," Mindy said. "Now go to sleep or Santa won't stop by. You know the rules."

Justin nodded and turned over, pulling the covers tight around his face.

"Goodnight, hun," Mindy said.

"Night, son," Ben added.

"Good night," Justin said.

They slipped out of his room and silently closed his door, the nightlight inside casting a warm glow.

"I was worried he'd have a hard time going to sleep, considering what happened last year," Ben said as they walked across the hall into their room.

"Kids are resilient. I only hope he never has to experience something like that again."

"I still don't understand any of it. It really happened, didn't it?"

Mindy nodded. She slipped off her shirt and pulled down her pajama bottoms, standing their completely naked.

"It did, but it's over now. Why don't you come here so we can make our own Christmas magic." She held out her hand to him, and Ben smiled, feeling himself grow erect. He took one step toward her, then was startled by a scratch at the door.

Ben let out a sigh. "I'll see what Justin needs. You might want to cover up. But...not too much." Ben winked and waited for Mindy to dress while the scratching continued at the door.

Ben opened the bedroom door. "Hey bud, what's going—" His voice caught in his throat. Three elves, all as mean and nasty looking as those from a year before, stood in his hallway. They were dressed in tattered green vests and pants, with pointy hats covered in dirt and grime. They snarled, exposing their long teeth. Saliva dripped off their fangs and onto the carpet.

"I told you," one of them said, raising a short arm with its bony claw pointed at him, "that blood would be spilled. Your mom was not enough. The bargain wasn't filled. You owed us your boy. Now we'll take it from you. A deal is a deal!"

The three elves lunged at him and dug their claws into his flesh. Ben cried out as the elves attacked. Mindy screamed. The last thing Ben remembered was his son opening his door and screaming. Blood splashed into Ben's eyes. *Run*, he thought. *Get away from here.* He hoped Justin was quick enough to flee from the elves. Burning pain tore through his body as the relentless attack continued. They were too much, too powerful to escape from. Ben closed his eyes, and he never saw Christmas again.

About the Stories

EVISCERATION LIBERATION

This story first appeared in *Camp Slasher Lake: Volume Two* released by Fedowar Press in 2022. This story features characters from my novels *Dreamwraith* and *Soul Eyes*.

GHOST FACTORY

This story was first published in the anthology *Executive Dread: Tales of Office Horror* in 2021 by Jolly Horror Press. It was a work-themed anthology, and I wanted to take a different spin on the drudgery of work.

KAPEROSA

This was written for my Patreon in the first quarter of 2024. I gave one of my Patrons the opportunity to not only name a character, but to give me all the details about the person. I took it a step further and let my Patron even dictate what kind of story it was going to be. My Patron, Teresa, gave me the details, and I took it from there. I loved how the story turned out!

THE GOD'S EYE

The God's Eye was originally published in the April 2017 issue of *SciFan Magazine*. The magazine has since shuttered, though the rights had already reverted back to me.

The story was my nod to the classic Frankenstein mythos, with a twist. The original kernel of the story came to me while in the shower, as most of my ideas do. I let it marinate for a few weeks and then wrote the story.

The title changed several times over the course of writing it, with the first version called "Bob's Big Night." I scrapped that and went with a more meaningful title. Other than the neural network present in the android, the title also refers to man's desire to supplant a higher power with their own intelligence, to create life from our own devices. How wise is that? I'll leave that for you to decide.

THE NIGHT I WAS BORN

This is sort of an origin story for my supernatural entity from my novel *Dreamwraith*. It was originally published in *99 Tiny Terrors: A Horror Anthology* by Pulse Publishing in 2022.

THE HOUSE ACROSS THE STREET

"The House Across the Street" was inspired by the house across from where I lived.

A year or two before we moved in to our former home, a young woman was kidnapped and found murdered in the fields just outside of town. In a small town like mine, it was headline news.

I was told by members of local law enforcement that the poor woman was held captive in the basement of the house across from me. Whether or not it's true, it has always bothered me to know something so horrific happened in such a nondescript neighborhood. I couldn't help but think of how many times people walked by that house while, unknown to them, real-life horror lived inside.

⸎

The Eternal Gift

I've really wanted to write a horror LitRPG story, and this was my first attempt. LitRPG is a wild genre of fiction that blends video games and RPGs (Role Playing Games) within a traditional novel-style delivery. They are creative and tons of fun to read. This story was my attempt at trying something close.

⸎

From Dust to Dust

Originally written for a themed anthology, I pulled the submission when the publishers decided to step back and it was given over to someone else. A historical piece set in the 1930s, "From Dust to Dust" was so much fun exploring the Ouija board and bringing it into a decade that is close to a century old by now.

⸎

ACHIEVEMENT UNLOCKED

This was originally published in *The Twilight Madhouse: Volume 1* back in 2017. This was an attempt to explore the dark side of video game addiction and how easy it is for some people to slip from reality to their warped version of it.

THE FOREVER CABIN

Inspired by a trip to the Grand Canyon back in 2021, this story was first drafted in the cabin described in the story in Williams, Arizona. Though we never experienced anything like the ghost in the story, it's always fun to let my imagination run wild.

BROTHER FRANCIS

This was originally published in *Head Blown: Extreme Horror Stories* back in the summer of 2023 as part of the Texas Author-Con. I wanted to try historical horror once again and decided to take it way back to the Middle Ages.

TWO DEATHS, ONE WIFE

No doubt you might associate the title with a more infamous video. This story is *not* a tribute to that, but I kinda liked the association with the title. It was first published in the D&T Publishing newsletter in October of 2022.

NECROTIC SANITATION

Ok, so this one. I was tempted to enter the Gross Out contest at AuthorCon in Williamsburg, VA, in April 2024. I wrote this story in a day and brought it with me to the Con but decided at the last minute not to enter it. It's vile and disgusting, but that's what a Gross Out story is! After attending the contest this year, I think I might give it another try at future Cons with other stories.

PEACE COMES FROM BLOOD, MILK AND COOKIES, AND CHRISTMAS STALKINGS

All three of these were published in *Dark X-Mas Holiday Drabbles: 100 Word Holiday Horror Stories* by Macabre Ladies Publishing in 2019. These stories are called drabbles, which are stories written in exactly one hundred words. That's tough to do!

LITTLE DEVILS

Originally written for a Christmas-themed horror anthology, it was not selected and I released it as its own chapbook in December of 2023. The cabin setting is inspired by a real one in Michigan that was built and owned by my stepdad's family. We used to love going there! Of course, nothing like what happened in the story occurred. At least not that I know.

Acknowledgments

Thank you for reading these stories. Their range is all over the place, and I hope you enjoyed them. If so, please consider leaving a review online. Those help readers discover my work.

I want to give thanks to a few people for making this book happen.

First of all, to all the publishers who took a chance on my stories: Thank you! I know they're inundated with submissions and to have mine chosen means a lot.

Secondly, I have to give a shout out to my Patrons from the Cellar! Thank you to Rebecca Rogers, Lisa Breanne, Dottie Sargent, Jason Artz, Mari Pittelman, Mary Trujillo, Rhonda Bobbitt, Stephanie Huddle, Charlotte Stevenson, Jyl Glenn, Molly Mix, Alicia Toothman, Dennis Smith, John Durgin, John Lynch, Megan Stockton, Candace Nola, Molly Mix, Savannah Fischer, and Steve Stred. I appreciate your friendship, and your support means more to me than I can ever say.

I wanna give a shout out to my cover designer, Matt Seff Barnes for this beautiful cover! I also have to thank Heather Larson for her edits. Thank you both for giving my book the polish it needs with the art outside and the words inside.

I have to give thanks to a few fellow authors that always have my back: John Lynch, John Durgin, Megan Stockton, and David Viergutz. Thank you for your friendship and for believing in me.

Finally, thanks to my family for your continued support and encouragement.

I appreciate all of you for your support and for reading my work. Without you, I'm screaming into an empty void.

-Jay

September 2024

ABOUT THE AUTHOR

Jay Bower is a horror author living outside St. Louis, MO in the forest of Southern Illinois. He spends his time reading, writing, and convincing his wife the dark stories he writes do not involve her.

For links to all his books, visit his website. There you can also get a free story for signing up to his reader list.

jaybowerauthor.com

facebook.com/jaybowerauthor
x.com/JayBowerAuthor
instagram.com/jaybowerauthor
tiktok.com/@jaybowerauthor

Also by Jay Bower

Horror Novels

The Dark Sacrifice

Soul Eyes

Useless Creatures

Dreamwraith

Slaughter Lake (Co-written with David Viergutz)

Master of Demons

Cadaverous

The Brownsville Nightmares (Collects The Dark Sacrifice, Soul Eyes, and Dreamwraith)

Every Time I Die

The Terror of Willow Falls

Eyebiter's Revenge (Novella)

Sleeper Train (Co-written with John Lynch)

Dead Blood Series

Dead Blood: Book One

Dead Blood: Book Two

Dead Blood: Book Three

Dead Blood: The Complete Series

Short Story Collections

Hanging Corpses

The Conservator's Collection: Derelict (with John Durgin and John Lynch)

Shadows from the Basement

Milton Keynes UK
Ingram Content Group UK Ltd.
UKHW041132151024
449742UK00017B/159/J